The Execution...
a step into N...
personal spa...

"Don't interfere with our evac. I'll shoot you dead if you do."

"You've got a white flag, soldier boy. Just remember there'll be no place for people like you in our new world."

"On my oath as a United States soldier, I'm duty bound to protect the Constitution from all enemies, foreign or domestic. Go back to your masters and tell them that I'm coming for them. And in my court there are no appeals."

Bolan would settle for a stalemate right now, but he knew there was still a whole war left to fight.

It was a war he'd have to win.

MACK BOLAN ®
The Executioner

DON PENDLETON'S
THE EXECUTIONER®
TRIGGER POINT

A GOLD EAGLE BOOK FROM
WORLDWIDE.

TORONTO • NEW YORK • LONDON
AMSTERDAM • PARIS • SYDNEY • HAMBURG
STOCKHOLM • ATHENS • TOKYO • MILAN
MADRID • WARSAW • BUDAPEST • AUCKLAND

First edition September 2000
ISBN 0-373-64262-8

Special thanks and acknowledgment to
Gerald Montgomery for his contribution to this work.

TRIGGER POINT

Printed in U.S.A.

These are the times that try men's souls. The summer
soldier and the sunshine patriot will, in this crisis, shrink
from the service of their country; but he that stands it *now*
deserves the...thanks of men and women. Tyranny, like hell,
is not easily conquered....

—Thomas Paine
The American Crisis

The idea that genetic history is the single most important
factor in determining who will rule and who will toil
goes back thousands of years. Some say we've evolved
out of that, that humankind is more mature. I've seen no
evidence of that. The Nazi movement of the twentieth
century argues to the contrary. This time if the Nazi
specter rises, I'll be there to challenge the enemy and
cart him off to hell.

—Mack Bolan

To the men and women of HHC, 2/135 Aviation Regiment in Aurora, Colorado. Continue to carry the torch of Liberty well into the twenty-first century.

1

Luxor, Pennsylvania

The voice on the other end of the line gave no hint as to its nationality or ethnic origin.

"Call your operator. Code Alpha 3 Zulu."

The words were a trigger, and a change came over the young woman like a fifty-degree drop in temperature. She was no longer Ashlee Hawkins, 3.5 GPA honor student and captain of her high-school cheerleading squad. She had no recollection of her church, her family, her friends. All she knew now was her mission.

Code Alpha 3 Zulu.

Ashlee was gone, and Alexis had taken her place. Alexis had been installed into Ashlee Hawkins's brain by a monster directly descended from the scientific dungeons of the Third Reich and imported into the American intelligence establishment during Operation Paperclip.

Alexis was the killer-elite personality, used for assassinations and general mayhem with the intent to sow chaos throughout the Land of the Free. Liza was another frequently accessed personality, the nymphomaniac porn-star persona. Liza was used for sexual blackmail and to satisfy the darkest appetites of her puppet masters. Yet another was for muling the drugs that financed their operations, while a fourth delivered secret messages between the members of the cryptocracy and their allies. There were others, all unknown to Ashlee Hawkins, Christ-loving high-school girl living in Luxor, Pennsylvania.

If Ashlee in the guise of Alexis, Liza or any of the others ever found the independence of thought to consciously picture the man who had unmade, then remade her, she would become confused and have flashbulb impressions of big-headed aliens with wraparound black eyes and cadaverous gray flesh. The process of beginning to remember the traumas suffered at the hands of human monsters would trigger programming that "remembered" aliens instead. If this ingeniously inspired bit of damage control was to ever weaken, there was always Code Green. The backup for the backup.

Ashlee was now neatly tucked away behind a hypnotically sealed wall in her brain. Alexis hung up the phone mechanically and turned to catch a reflection of herself in the glass of the microwave-oven door.

She didn't see her blond hair, flowing to her hips, pulled tight into a long, single tail that roped behind her. Instead, she saw Alexis's raven-black hair. She didn't see frosty blue eyes or teen-queen good looks. She saw crocodile eyes staring back. She wasn't wearing a school letter sweater, and the perky little breasts beneath were cold now and goosefleshed inside the armored brassiere she saw reflected back.

She was a Valkyrie, with steel breast cups under a chain-mail tank top. Alexis smirked with Kewpie-doll red lips.

The doorbell rang, and she responded like a Pavlovian dog, gliding to the front door without a thought to what she was doing or why. She opened it, and a grinning man in black stood on the porch. He wore a black suit, black shirt, black tie, black fedora pulled low over his forehead, and black sunglasses veiled his eyes.

"Aquarius thought you might need this," he said.

Alexis took the rifle case from the man she saw as a towering gray alien, set it at her feet so she could sign off on an imaginary shipping receipt. She handed the thin-air receipt back and closed the door, thinking everything was quite in order.

She knelt and opened the rifle case. Inside was a new AK-47 assault rifle, glistening with gun oil. It smelled of solvent and steel with an undercurrent of death that flushed her with crazy desires for sex and blood. Three 30-round banana magazines nestled beside the rifle, along with a lethal 9 mm Glock handgun for mop-up.

Her trained-killer's eyes noted with approval that the serial numbers on both weapons had been ground away, preventing law-enforcement agencies from tracing them back to her or her unseen puppet masters.

She slung the rifle over her shoulder, gathered the loaded magazines and tucked the Glock into the waistband of her jeans. Then she left the house and headed to the green Volvo station wagon, her mother's car, parked in the driveway.

Alexis opened the passenger-side door and deposited the assault rifle below the gearshift between the front seats, then stacked the three magazines on the passenger seat before closing the door. She pulled the keys out of her pocket, went to the driver's side and slid behind the wheel.

She had an appointment to keep with a festering nest of godless Communists.

RICH LAWSON, Tommy Knutson and Ryan Hildebrant smoked cigarettes as they leaned against the chain-link fence that separated the athletic fields from the student parking lot of Luxor High School. Since the antismoking lobby had swayed policy makers to their side, high schools in the county were forbidden to allow student-smoking areas. The official smoking area had been shut down. The unofficial smoking area immediately sprang up five minutes later on the other side of the parking lot against the fence line of the athletic fields.

As long as the butts were policed up, the faculty made every attempt to look the other way.

The topic of discussion today revolved around the latest intrusion of the social engineers from Washington. These "do-gooders" were trying to ram mandatory urinalysis of all students attending schools receiving any kind of federal funding.

"We need a new amendment to the Constitution," Rich quipped.

Tommy blew out a cloud of blue smoke. "Say what?"

"Yeah, a new amendment. One which'll make very clear that all of us have the inalienable right to put into our bodies whatever we feel like putting there—nicotine, THC or fruit and vegetables. The fucking Feds have no jurisdiction over our internal bodies.''

As Rich half listened to his friend's tirade, he watched a green Volvo park near the front of the main school building. His eyes widened as he saw Ashlee Hawkins get out of the car and put on her school letter jacket, then circle the rear of the station wagon to open the passenger door.

His eyes narrowed as he watched her methodically stuff curved black objects into the pockets of her jacket. What they were didn't register until she pulled the assault rifle out of the car and stuck one of the objects into the weapon, yanking back on the charging handle to put a round into the chamber. Ashlee test sighted the weapon to her left and right, then, satisfied that she was ready, jogged from the station wagon toward the front entrance of the school.

Rich's mind couldn't quite believe the signals his eyes continued to send. The captain of the cheerleading squad was about to fire on her own school with an automatic assault rifle.

He threw his half-smoked cigarette aside and screamed, "Oh, my God! She's got a rifle!''

Rich sprinted across the parking lot, arms pistoning, on an intercept course with the girl he secretly loved. With the girl he thought he had figured out.

ALEXIS WENT TO ONE KNEE at the curb, bringing the assault rifle into target acquisition. Casualty number one was Assistant Principal Richard Maddox. He was rushing out the school entrance to intercept Ashlee Hawkins before she entered the school with a firearm. The thought that she might put three high-velocity 7.62 mm rounds into his face never occurred to him; he was sure that all he had to do was speak loudly and authoritatively to the girl and the aura of his position in the school would do the rest.

He was just across the threshold of the door, opening his mouth to verbally disarm the girl when she fired her weapon. His head snapped back, cored by the first metal-jacketed slug that left the rifle's barrel. The next two rounds had no more excuse than an itchy trigger finger.

She sprinted into the school's entry foyer, jumping over Maddox's body to get through the doorway. The buttstock of the rifle was still pressed aggressively into her shoulder, her cheek welded to the weapon behind the open sights, both eyes scanning for her next target.

The main office was directly ahead. The floor-to-ceiling glass walls afforded an unobstructed view of Richard Maddox's violent exit from life to the women clerking in there; they stared, dumbfounded, at Ashlee, all eyes and mouth through the glass barrier that separated predator from prey.

Alexis smiled at the four horrified women over the top of the Kalashnikov before picking them off left to right like birds in a cage. The rifle sounded like bombs going off in the building, reverberating through the school like a seismic death sentence. A door opened in the office, and Principal Bevins poked out his head to see what was happening. He spotted the four bloodied women on the floor dead or dying before he saw Ashlee Hawkins drawing a bead on him through the shattered glass wall.

For his age, he was still quite agile. He pulled his head back just as three rounds chewed the door frame. He slammed his office door and locked it.

She didn't have time to waste on Bevins. There were other fish to fry. Alexis stalked across the foyer, angling for the main hallway, when the voice behind her spun her.

"Ashlee! For God's sake, what are you doing?"

It was Rich Lawson. She hesitated, almost breaking the trance, fighting to recall why this boy's face had meaning to her, stirring up the kind of emotions that Alexis felt only when thinking of murder and death. Her programming settled the matter with a crimson jolt of rage and pain.

"I am Alexis!"

Rich threw himself to the floor as the bullet drilled his left shoulder like a red-hot poker. His reactive dive saved him. Had he been standing upright one heartbeat longer, the youth would have been victim number six that day. The impact picked him up in middive and swatted him through the glass door to land on cold concrete in a glittering rain of razored jewels.

She waited only long enough to confirm that her target was down and wasn't getting up.

Alexis dropped the magazine, letting it clatter to the tiled floor, and slammed a fresh one home, then released the bolt to cycle the first round off the top.

She sprinted down the main hallway in search of fresh blood.

CONSTABLE JIM CROWLEY pounded down the science hallway, his service revolver drawn and ready. The handgun was a Smith & Wesson Model 66 .357 Magnum, with a six-inch barrel. Crowley had been concluding his drug-education presentation to Ms. Reingold's fifth-period biology class when the shooting started at the entrance of the school.

That had been about twenty seconds ago.

Another volley of shots rang out ahead, cutting several screams short, and the ricochets whined like lethal insects.

At the T-junction connecting the science hallway to the main breezeway, Crowley pressed his back against the last locker from the corner and listened, both hands gripping his pistol. He heard wet shoe-scuffing on the polished concrete, as if heels were trying to dig in for purchase but weren't getting anywhere due to the presence of a slick lubricant. Something like oil or blood… His stomach rolled, knowing what that was all about, what it meant to the person down there now heartbeats away from the last breath, the final darkness.

The quavery "Please don't" belonged to a girl, crazy with fear, lucid with the knowledge of what was coming next.

But not if Crowley could help it.

He pivoted around the corner, raising the pistol, and the shock of who he saw standing over the bleeding form left him gasping.

"Ashlee?" was all he could say.

Jim Crowley had known her since she was in diapers. Her folks were good people, and Ashlee had been a good girl—overall. She'd had some trouble with teen rebellion, running with the wrong crowd, but her folks had done the right thing, sending her away for a year to a Christian hard-love boot camp in Louisiana. Ashlee had come back a model of Christian behavior, someone the community could marvel over.

The shock of truth caused him to hesitate in the heartbeat that would have made the difference.

When she heard that name again, her eyes shifted from the whimpering girl at her feet. The AK-47 swung up and locked on with no hesitation. Her battle drills were perfect. Nothing could make them crash.

They both fired at each other at the same time across twenty feet.

The 7.62 mm round cored Crowley's chest center mass. He was only peripherally aware of being swatted off his feet by an invisible locomotive. He flew backward in a dreamscape; he didn't feel his body impact against the wall lockers on the other side of the hall or his slide to the floor.

In his last moments of awareness, he was conscious of seeing Ashlee bucked off her feet and the AK-47 tossed to the left of her windmilling pantomime to the floor. The .357 round had caught her square in the left breast, mushrooming, spraying tissue and blood behind her.

She sat up after hitting the floor, looking more like a malfunctioning android than a gunshot victim as she pulled a Glock pistol from the waistband of her jeans and brought it up.

He drunkenly slapped the floor around him, lamely trying to palm the pistol that lay seven feet out of reach. His dying instincts were true; it was his interpretation that was wrong.

She wasn't pulling the backup piece to finish him off. The Glock was for her.

Her voice was scoured of all feeling and emotion.

"Code Green," she stated.

Crowley watched as Ashlee pressed the 9 mm Glock pistol into her forehead and pulled the trigger. Her dead torso flopped back in the raining wreckage of her own head.

Then he did the final fadeout to black.

Midland, Texas

THE BROADCAST MEDIA didn't make their bread and butter from good news. The story was running on all networks, preempting scheduled programming with news anchors spewing rumor and speculation, cutting to interviews with behavior experts and bureau chiefs reporting from Capitol Hill. There had been three separate incidents, each shockingly familiar—one lone teen with an assault weapon had slaughtered dozens of innocents.

The unanimous media slant was uncanny. The sheer improbability of three copycat incidents occurring on the same day went completely unaddressed. The specter of gun control was raising its ugly head yet again.

And it was a concerted, coordinated effort.

Democratic senator from Texas, John Mannix, watched the Fox broadcast, then clicked to ABC. It was simply incredible the way the networks were suddenly all singing the same tune. Nationwide polls were pulling for more crackdowns on the availability of assault rifles.

Mannix snorted with contempt. Simply tell the sheep what to think, and they'd spit back what was expected. He'd just been on the phone with his D.C. staff. An "emergency" session of Congress was being called to vote on one-thousand-plus pages of legislation to address this crisis. Mannix knew better. One thousand pages of legislation couldn't just spring into existence within hours of the tragedies it was tailored to combat. That legislation had been sitting in the wings, waiting for the manufactured events that would justify its fast-track ratification. Like these tragedies—a concerted, coordinated effort.

Statistical probability said that such a set of events was impossible. Senator Mannix cast his lot with statistical probability. These events were anything but random. They were communicating with those who knew how to read the signs.

The time was near.

Mannix loved his country, and her darkest hours were at hand. He thought about George Washington's prophetic vision—the twilight of the Republic and the Sons of Liberty rallying to the call and taking her out of harm's way. There weren't many Sons of Liberty left, he thought bitterly. The Founding Fathers were no longer visionaries in the eyes of the American public. They were painted now as a bunch of white racists with odd notions about civil liberties.

His party was full of those socialist traitors and sellouts, and yet he continued to declare himself a

Democrat. He may be the only one left, but he was going to keep alive the Democratic ideal he'd long been championing.

Though Mannix was an old warhorse, he was far from being ready to be put out to pasture. He would have politically reclassified himself a libertarian years ago, but he was enough of a player to know that such a move would have been political suicide. He maintained a power post in Washington, D.C. that he couldn't afford to jeopardize, not this late in the game. He had a stranglehold on the chairmanship of the Senate Intelligence Oversight Committee, and that was still his ace in the hole. The enemy was deeply entrenched inside the nation's intelligence and military-industrial complex, just as Eisenhower had warned, and as chairman he could keep an eye on the progress the enemy was making. He'd become quite adept at interpreting the doctored reports and assessments that were forwarded to his committee for oversight and review.

He kept his mouth shut and looked for weakness.

Mannix sat in the big green leather wingback chair in the study of his ranch house in the oil lands outside Midland. The room was decorated in honor to the rich culture of the most unique state in the Union. It was a harmonious blending of Western Americana and Spanish-Indian influences. The Texas flag was mounted on rich green felt backing and framed tastefully, hanging above the panoramic bay windows that dominated the background behind his desk. The walls were white adobe stucco, adorned with the heads of prize bucks in key areas around the perimeter of the room.

The double oak doors opened, and Secret Service Agent Anthony James entered the room, holding a cordless phone.

"It's the White House, Senator."

Mannix motioned him over to his side and took the phone.

"Thank you, Anthony."

Agent James nodded and retreated, closing the doors behind him.

It was his old friend, another Democrat of the old breed, who held the highest executive post in the land.

"Yes, sir. What can I do for you today?"

"Hello, John. I hope I'm not interrupting something more important."

"I'm just following the latest assault on the Bill of Rights on the television."

"The Bill of Rights is on the endangered list, John. This new legislation that's fast-tracking will be the nail in the coffin. And I couldn't veto it if I wanted to."

"For what it's worth, sir, I'm voting against it."

"Have you read it?"

"Don't have to, sir. I already know what it aims to do. Abolish the Second Amendment for all practical purposes."

"And the Fourth," the Man added.

"And habeas corpus and the concept that we are all innocent until proved guilty."

"I'm always amazed at the quality and accuracy of your information."

"I make it my business."

"I can't veto this, John," the Man repeated, almost apologetically, "but I think it's time I let you in on a little secret. I had hoped that they might slip up along the line somewhere, that the hot light of day might shine into their shadow empire. But you and I both know that they've got the media sewn up tight. They're ready to dissolve the Republic. I can't officially bring this asset into our loop. I'm being watched too closely. But you can."

Mannix leaned forward in his favorite chair, taking the bait.

"Give it to me, sir."

The President went on to tell Mannix about a certain man who was a true patriot, a man who would fight to the death to uphold truth and justice, and the ideals of the United States of America.

Something Mannix hadn't felt in many months now swept over his soul. The winds of hope.

The Republic wasn't finished yet.

The Man gave him the patriot's phone number, told him how to make the contact, wished him good luck and hung up.

2

The white Lincoln Continental stretch limousine sat on the concrete apron in front of the huge roll-away doors of Hangar 18. The runway system of the former Air Force base was still intact, though not maintained. The west Texas desert was slowly reclaiming the concrete strips one crack at a time. A cold wind was blowing in from the north, lifting loose topsoil and dead vegetation into the atmosphere. Ominous purple clouds roiled above on a low ceiling. It would probably rain, and if the temperature dropped enough, the rain would turn to ice.

Mannix felt the low bass thump in his bones before the noise became audible. He turned his head in the direction of the throb and leaned forward so he could look out the tinted glass for the approaching aircraft. He scanned the horizon.

The helicopter skimmed the sage and scrag oak on a low-level intercept with the waiting limo. As the aircraft closed the gap, Mannix recognized the gunship: an AH-64 Apache attack chopper. Fully armed rocket pods and miniguns bristled from under the nose and stabilizer fins.

The gunship flew straight to the loading zone and flared to a hover forty yards off Mannix's car door. The Apache touched down lightly, almost elegantly, and the rotors went into an idle. The pilot was keeping the engine running, which was obviously a security protocol.

A tall man in a black flight suit disembarked while removing his flight helmet, leaving it in the aircraft. He climbed down to the apron and went under the stabilizer fin and opened a panel on a footlocker-like box built flush against the fuselage. He pulled out two heavy-looking bags. One was a standard Army-issue duffel bag, and the other was a navy-blue rifle case made out of ballistic nylon.

Mannix got out of the car as his Secret Service agent did the same from the driver's compartment. The senator stepped away from the open door to allow his guest access to the interior.

The big man strolled up to the senator and placed the ordnance bags at this feet. Mannix saw that the man was wearing a Velcro nameplate on the left breast of his flight suit. Col. Pollack, R. USA.

The senator offered his hand and the big man took it.

"Welcome to Texas, Colonel."

Mack Bolan nodded and eyed the Secret Service agent, who eyed him back.

"Secret Service or private muscle?" the big man asked.

"Secret Service," Agent James answered. "And you?"

"Justice Department."

Mannix stepped into the exchange.

"Your nameplate says U.S. Army."

"I'm attached to Justice in an advisory capacity."

"I see."

Bolan waited a few heartbeats. "What's this all about, Senator? I put an important piece of business on hold just to be here."

"Will you join me for a short drive? What I have to tell you will take a little time. But I assure you that I wouldn't have requested your review of this situation if it wasn't of immense importance. Why don't you tell that flyboy of yours to shut down the bird and join us for a ride?"

Mannix noticed the throat mike affixed to the big man's collar.

The soldier touched the throat mike and said, "Jack, I'm taking a ride with the senator. I want you to shadow us from above. Report anything unusual. You know the drill."

"Roger. I invented the drill."

"All right, Senator. Let's go."

Mannix indicated the open door with a sweeping gesture. Bolan hefted his bags and placed them in the middle of the spacious interior before climbing into the car. The senator followed him in and closed the door. Up front, Agent James was already behind the wheel and starting the vehicle.

"Let's get out of town, Anthony."

The Secret Service agent nodded. "Yes, sir."

The white limo rolled off the apron and around the hangar, pursued by the Apache gunship. Grimaldi kept the chopper about fifty feet off the ground, to the left rear of the car below. With the gunship in tow, nobody would be foolhardy enough to try to attack the car.

The white limo with its escort headed south, out of town and into the canyons of the surrounding desert.

ALMOST TEN MINUTES had passed since the senator picked up his passenger at the Big Spring Industrial Park, and other than the obligatory pleasantries and handshakes upon meeting, there had been no conversation. The colonel just sat there, sizing things up and waiting for the senator to make the opening move.

Mannix looked out the tinted glass to his left at the sun-bleached dunes and landscape, dark under the brewing storm. He returned his gaze to his guest and cut to the chase.

"I have no doubt that you love your country, Colonel Pollack. That oath you took to protect the Constitution was more like a marriage vow, wasn't it?"

"I don't believe in dancing around an issue or playing games with the truth. I'm laying my cards on the table faceup, Senator. No surprises. I trust that you are a similar kind of man."

Mannix nodded.

"Okay, Senator. I'm tracking."

"Several lifetimes ago, before I watched them murder a President, I would have frowned gravely upon what I am doing here today."

"What is it you're doing today, Senator?"

"Please, call me John."

Bolan nodded.

"I'm doing God's work for Him since He seems to have taken a vacation since the beginning of World War II. The law no longer dispenses impartial justice. The law is wax in their hands, a clever weave that they hide behind while declaring themselves above prosecution, above common ethics and morality. They do as they please, and they aspire to lord over every clump of dirt on this planet. These men are of a breed I'm sure you have an intimate, working knowledge of."

The Executioner merely nodded.

"I've heard from the President that you are a man who has stepped outside the law, worked outside the law to see that some of the monsters meet the justice they deserve. Officially, I can't go after these people or even attempt to expose them. They're outside the law. But so are you."

"Who are they?"

"They refer to themselves as COMCON."

"A code name?"

Mannix frowned while shaking his head.

"No, more of an acronym. The Committee to Suspend the U.S. Constitution. COMCON. The sons of bitches really do think that they're untouchable, calling themselves something like that. They are heavily entrenched in all the federal intelligence and police agencies, and FEMA, the Federal Emergency Management Agency, is a creation entirely theirs, legislated into existence by a Congress full of good yes men."

The Executioner didn't comment but waited for more.

Mannix spread his arms wide, apparently to encompass all creation.

"They're all over the three branches of government, in the think tanks, the policy circles, the defense industry and research and development."

"That's a pretty tall order."

"No, it's the twilight of the great American experiment, I'm afraid. It'll all be over by 2001, 2010 at the latest."

Mannix knew just by watching that Pollack wasn't sold on any of this. He'd yet to give the soldier anything concrete to be sold on. Some subjects had to be approached with preparatory information and preambles, and he hadn't even scratched the surface of the subject yet.

"John, do you know what an order of battle is?"

Mannix nodded. "It's intelligence on an enemy that details their organization, equipment, tactics, morale and so on."

"Exactly. That's what I'm going to need before I can dig into any of your claims."

"That would be difficult due to the fact that they have no centralized command structure and operate like terrorist cells. I imagine that somewhere there must be a group of planners that know the big picture and the identities of all the cells, but that's information that I haven't been privy to. You'd probably find that bunch inside Storm Mountain, where FEMA maintains a nerve center to take over the government of this country in the event of a national emergency. Do you realize, through executive order, FEMA has been given the powers to suspend the Constitution, institute martial law, seize all business operations and organize the population into work camps if the President were to ever declare a serious national emergency?''

Bolan had heard of FEMA. His impression was that the agency was some kind of federal disaster-assistance corps. His brushes with the extreme right-wing militias had exposed him to their paranoid theories about growing federal "tyranny," and FEMA was a central bugaboo to these people. He wondered what side of the political pasture the senator stood in.

"Senator, by chance, are you a sympathizer with certain right-wing-patriot causes?''

The old Democrat laughed heartily at the suggestion.

"No, but some of the things they're squeaking about aren't half off the mark.''

"I see.''

"You know, the patriot movement's most glaring mistake in its theories is referring to COMCON as a 'Communist' conspiracy. It's no more of Communist origin than I am. I'm talking fascism here. They're a bunch of fascists, and they set up shop in our government, in our intelligence agencies at the end of World War II at the invitation of our own people. You ever heard of Operation Paperclip?''

"Is that what it was called?''

"Then you're familiar with what this program accomplished?''

"The pardoning and integration of top-ranking Nazis into the Allied anti-Communist cold war that followed the end of the big war. Yeah, I'm familiar with it.''

A recent campaign had led Bolan to Germany and into a head-long confrontation with a surviving Nazi conspiracy, the same pagan black-magic order that had erected the Third Reich on blood and will alone. The Thule Society. Bolan sensed an ominous connection between the Thule and this COMCON organization the senator was warning him of.

Bolan fired a shot in the dark.

"Would this have anything to do with the Thule Society?"

"Oh, I think so. The Thulists came over here with the rest of that SS trash. The Thule Society was the true source of power behind Hitler. They were a chilling bunch of lunatics, worshiping the Old Ones and using the slaughter of the Final Solution as one gigantic, ongoing human sacrifice in honor of their monster gods. Sounds like something right out of Lovecraft."

Bolan's thoughts were drawn to Heinrich Heine, the ninety-four-year-old fossil of the Third Reich he'd matched wits with in Germany. The wheelchair-bound Heine had surprised Bolan with his sheer presence, a crackling field of pure personal power that radiated off the feeble old bones. That man had a very real power that seemed to affect the physical atmosphere surrounding his body. It was something that could be felt on the skin like static electricity in the air.

Bolan didn't know about Satan and God, but if ultimate metaphysical Evil had a point of origin other than the human heart, Heinrich Heine and his Thulists had made contact with that source, aligned their minds and hearts with that black rhythm and channeled that evil force into their bodies for storage like human capacitors.

The captured intel in the wake of the German campaign hinted that Heine's operation had established a vast global network. Bolan couldn't ignore the senator's claims without first looking into them. The similarities between the Thulist agenda and what Mannix was describing couldn't be a coincidence.

"It sounds like something I've encountered before. I assume you have a place for me to start looking."

"Yes, absolutely. Two days ago, in fact."

Mannix watched the man cock an eyebrow.

"Tell me, Colonel. How likely is it that three different teenagers, in three separate parts of the country, will all spontaneously decide to pick up the same make of assault rifle and massacre dozens of innocents before conveniently committing suicide?"

"It's theoretically possible."

"Sure, it's theoretically possible. But in the real world, I'm not going to hold my breath waiting for it to happen."

"Teenagers kill people every day of the week."

"But three copycat incidents on the same day? And one of the perps was a female. Hell, they practically signed their names to this one. Any good criminal behaviorist will tell you that this isn't the kind of crime a female would commit. How do females commit suicide?"

Bolan thought about it.

"By cutting their wrists or ODing."

"Exactly. Males swallow a gun barrel. Females,

as a rule, don't take care of their problems by picking up an AK-47 and shooting up the school yard or local McDonald's. That's a male act of violence. COMCON is being blatant now. They're telling us that they can make anyone do anything they want, anywhere, at anytime."

Mannix had Bolan's attention.

"If you're wondering what the purpose for all of this is, it's very simple to see. What has been the unanimous media slant on these tragic events?"

"Gun control."

"Yes, absolutely. Private ownership of firearms, any kind of firearms, is the linchpin in the entire Bill of Rights. It's the guarantee that keeps the government honest. If the monopoly on force lies exclusively in the hands of the government—"

"Then there is no check against the government becoming a tyranny," Bolan finished for him.

"Exactly. Why are they targeting assault rifles? Statistically, assault rifles are used in less than one percent of the violent crimes committed in America. Handguns are the overwhelming weapon of choice in any gun-related crime. Why assault rifles?"

The answer was obvious.

"Because assault rifles are civilian versions of military weapons. Their availability guarantees that the general population has similar armament as the military."

Mannix nodded like a proud teacher listening to a gifted pupil put it all together.

"And if the common folks are armed just like the military, and if the government ever tried to use the military to force a dictatorship down our throats,

well, it's going to be one hell of a shootin' match—
thanks to the Second Amendment.''

"Can you prove any of this?"

"Oh, hell yes. What do all three of those kids
have in common?"

Bolan waited for the answer.

"Every one of them spent a year in northern Louisiana at a fundamentalist-Christian behavior-
modification camp called Tranquillity Base. All that
fundamentalist crap is just window dressing to lull
worried Christian parents into donating their rebel-
lious teenagers to these mind rapers for forty thousand dollars up front.''

"Where is this place?"

"Louisiana. But relax, son. This is going to be
my treat. I've got several concerned grandparents
and in-laws filing suit to get kids out of that cess-
pool. So many questions have been raised, in fact, I
have no choice but to launch an official fact-finding
mission over these allegations. I was hoping you
might tag along with me on this posing as one of
my Secret Service boys. What do you say?"

The Executioner sat back in his seat.

"Let's go to Louisiana."

HOMER GUMP CAME OUT of the blind curve a little
too sharp and fast and he started to let the 1991 Olds
Bravada drift into the oncoming lane while the vehicle straightened. His wife, Lillian, saw the other
car a nanosecond before he did and screamed as her
husband yanked the wheel back. The kids were
screaming from the back seat and the huge white

whale of a car coming at them took a darting evasive maneuver onto the shoulder to avoid the Bravada.

In the wake of the near collision, an Apache gunship dropped from the sky and tracked the SUV with its lethal nose guns, looking over the Gumps for anything that resembled hostile intent. Gump was an Army Guard veteran, and he knew enough about the hunter-killer helicopters to know that anything falling into its gun sights didn't have a hope. That chain gun in the nose would wipe the Bravada off the face of the planet.

Gump kept driving.

In the rearview mirror, he watched the white limo tear off the shoulder and disappear around the blind corner. The Apache lingered an extra thirty seconds, weapons systems locked on to the tailgate of the Bravada, then disengaged to pursue the limo.

Gump gulped and sighed with relief. He pulled the SUV off the blacktop and onto the crushed rock of the shoulder, then glanced at his crotch to make sure he hadn't soiled himself during all that excitement.

His two children were crying, and as Gump turned to speak to them something else caught his eye, something strange and unexpected.

"What the hell is going on?" he muttered.

A large sand dune stood at about the two-o'clock position from the passenger-side doors of the Bravada. Gump estimated that the dune was about twenty yards high. Two helicopters, flat black in color, had popped up over the top of the dune, noses pointed in the direction that the limousine and Apache were traveling. Gump figured that he was within a hundred yards of the two helicopters, so he knew that distance wasn't the obstacle preventing him from identifying the model and nomenclature of the two gunships hovering over the dune.

Lillian said, "Oh, look, kids! Look at the helicopters! Honey, what kind of helicopters are those? Are they two of ours?"

Gump didn't answer.

He liked to think that he had a pretty good knowledge of Army helicopter inventories. These two birds were something that *Aviation and Space Weekly* had no knowledge of. The black helicopters looked like a cross between a Black Hawk and Blue Thunder. The designers had obviously set out to incorporate the best of a utility helicopter's features with that of an attack helicopter, so that the bird could bomb the hell out of a target *and* drop troops. Two missions, one piece of equipment.

Gump's curiosity about the strange helicopters' make and model gave way to a dawning dread that washed icy waves through his being.

"Gee, honey, aren't those helicopters real quiet?" Lillian asked.

The two black gunships dipped and darted down the road, toward the blind curve.

Something sparked in Gump's mind, and he went into action. He twisted in his seat, shifted the transmission to Drive and stomped the accelerator while spinning the wheel aggressively to the left. The Bravada spit gravel and hooked a tight U-turn. He kept the accelerator down as he straightened, let off a bit to take the blind corner and stepped on it again.

Lillian gasped, and the kids screamed.

"Homer, are you out of your mind? What are you doing?"

"Do you know what those were, Lillian?" Gump asked. "Those were real goddamn United Nations Communist black helicopters! I'm going to see what those Communist bastards are doing in west Texas!"

Gump maneuvered through another bend in the road and remembered the camera.

"Lillian, get the blasted camera out! We need pictures of this! Proof that these Commies are right here in our backyards!"

Getting good photographic evidence of black helicopters was like trying to get a good, clear picture of a UFO. Gump was thinking about how much money he might be able to make with a good set of pictures of genuine New World Order strike choppers in action. *Soldier of Fortune, Penthouse* or, at the very least, *Sightings* would pay a significant amount of cash to be the first to release the hard-hitting photographs. And then the UN would have a lot of explaining to do. It could blow the lid off the whole conspiracy. Gump could see all these possibilities and more.

He just had to get the pictures first.

THE HELICOPTERS DIDN'T CONFORM to anything in the U.S. or NATO inventories. No country in the world had anything like these birds. The aircraft were roughly the same size as a CH-47 Chinook and could carry the same payload. The similarities ended there. They could maintain a top speed of two hundred knots, outmaneuver an Apache and were invisible on radar. The choppers were armed with rocket pods mounted under two stabilizer fins and one 20 mm Vulcan cannon in the nose.

The birds were called AeroDeth by the engineers who drafted their lethal lines. They had no markings or registry numbers anywhere on the fuselage, and were painted matte black. The mainstream media scoffed at the rumors of their existence. The underground media knew they were out there.

What had originally been briefed as a simple snatch op had just become more complicated. The unexpected presence of the AH-64 flying escort for the senator's limo demanded a last-minute change of plan. The Apache had to be dealt with before they could even think about taking what they'd come for. A new plan was quickly decided upon between the two pilots on the secure channel without bringing their command and control into the loop on this new development. The longer he could be kept uninvolved in the pilots' problem solving, the better.

The new plan was simple in concept, but tricky in execution. The pilot of the Apache was the variable that could monkey wrench the entire operation. The pilots were going to separate, isolate, then annihilate the obstacle.

THE PROXIMITY ALARMS went off in the cockpit at the same time that the radar readout was tracking multiple bogies, closing fast, originating about two hundred yards to the left flank of his rear sector. Jack Grimaldi knew that the radar contacts were air-to-air missiles. Somebody was trying to blow him out of the sky.

The identity of his attacker or attackers remained unknown: the radar screen wasn't tracking a launch-point target at all. According to radar, those missiles just popped into existence a heartbeat ago, armed and locked on to the AH-64. The enemy had to be employing some form of stealth technology to be scattering radar like that.

Grimaldi didn't have time to debate it.

"Striker," Grimaldi reported, "I'm under attack. I'm going to have to abandon station to shake them."

Then the Stony Man pilot threw the Apache into a dive as the missiles corrected for the target's sudden change of course and dropped altitude to continue pursuit.

AGENT ANTHONY JAMES blinked to make sure that he wasn't hallucinating. Reflexively he took his foot off the accelerator, and the big Lincoln coasted over the crest of the small bluff surrounded by black-and-tan mesas. Fifty yards ahead were two squads of black-clad, heavily armed troops with a helicopter hovering above them.

James wasn't at a loss for something to do. His training kicked in without conscious thought. The scene ahead spelled nothing but trouble, and his job was to keep the senator out of it. He slammed on the brakes while spinning the wheel at the same time, throwing the heavy vehicle into a classic boot-legger's turn. When the Lincoln twisted about 180 degrees and faced the opposite direction, he stomped the accelerator to the floor.

The abrupt maneuver caught the two passengers

in the back completely off guard. The intercom squawked and the senator's voice growled, "Anthony, what the hell's going on? Colonel Pollack says his pilot is under attack."

James didn't bother to reply over the intercom. He lowered the soundproof partition that separated the driver's compartment from the rear.

"We've got about two dozen armed troops and a nasty-looking helicopter back there. I didn't want to stick around to see what their intentions were."

"What?"

The senator turned in his seat to look out the rear window. His passenger was already there.

"That helicopter's on an intercept," Bolan stated. "We'll never outrun it."

James called over his shoulder, eyeing the speedometer, which was pinned at seventy miles per hour. Too slow. "I'm open to suggestions!"

"Just keep gunning it," Bolan replied. "I'll take care of the bird."

James gunned it.

To the Executioner, the sudden turn of events was nothing but confirmation. If the senator's claims were little more than crackpot fantasy, they wouldn't be in the middle of an ambush. The enemy's presence told Bolan that the senator was under close surveillance, which meant that somebody didn't like what Mannix was keeping tabs on and were about to take action.

Bolan unzipped the weapons case and pulled out two halves of a serious-looking weapon, mating the lower receiver to the upper receiver, and thumbing two pins home that held the sections together. The weapon was an M-16 A-2 with an M-203 grenade launcher riding beneath it. Bolan didn't bother slamming a 30-round magazine into the assault rifle. The chopper was probably armored, and the 5.56 mm bullets wouldn't even mar the paint job. He pulled out an assault vest heavy with projectiles for the M-203 and selected a high-explosive airburst round. He opened the weapon's breech and slid the round home.

The strange black helicopter was already pulling in front of them as the Executioner flipped up the front blade sight for the grenade launcher.

"That helicopter is down in front of us!" James reported. "And there's another one of those bastards waiting!"

"Go onto the shoulder if you have to!" Bolan ordered. "Just get around them!"

The pursuing chopper's cannon cut loose with a three-second burst, and the nose of the Lincoln disappeared in fire and smoke. The bulletproof windshield yielded, and James gasped as he was hit. The heavy car veered sharply to the right, left the road and began its agonizing death spiral in billowing clouds of sunbaked dirt.

The second AeroDeth helicopter banked away from the kill zone, dipping toward the ground to finish off what remained of the Apache gunship after the missiles took their toll.

Bolan held on to the door handle and waited for the limo to stop moving before he made his play.

He was only going to have one shot, and it had to count.

"TARGET DISABLED," the pilot reported curtly.

C and C's voice rang inside his helmet.

"What about the precious cargo? Do you have a visual on the precious cargo?"

"Negative. I'm still waiting for the dirt to settle."

"I want a visual, mister. Now! How copy?"

"I copy! Out!"

God, C and C was a miserable son of a bitch.

The pilot nosed the bird closer and let the rotor wash siphon off the mucky cloud that was clinging to the disabled vehicle like a funeral pyre. He could see movement down there. Somebody was alive in the rear—

"I see...shit!"

The rear door facing the hovering gunship popped open, and a big grim man dressed in black jumped out and shouldered the last thing the pilot had been briefed to expect: massive resistance. He tried to fire and pull up at the same time, but the doomsday numbers had gone sour for him. There was a puff of smoke from a tube anchored beneath the barrel of the assault rifle, and a small black object arced upward with a gray contrail wisping behind it. That high-explosive hardball tracked up and behind the cockpit bubble, detonating inside the main rotors.

The pilot's world went to hell in a nova burst of white-hot light and angry thunder.

GRIMALDI PULLED the gunship out of the dive and immediately went into a sharp course adjustment to his ten o'clock. He willed more speed from the chopper, jockeying for the V between two mesas. The four missiles were within seventy yards. Taller scrub oaks were intermittently scraping the belly of the attack helicopter as Grimaldi held the aircraft as close to nap of the earth as he could get without uprooting major chunks of the landscape with the landing gear. The V between the two mesas loomed up, and he was in.

The Stony Man Farm pilot arbitrarily selected the mesa to his left to pinwheel around. The mesa was shaped like a kidney and looked like the more probable of the two to offer good sheer cliff faces that he hoped to use as impromptu impact areas. Failing that, he was prepared to fly as wildly around and over the top of the weathered rock as a pilot of his skill was capable, until he ran the rockets out of fuel, falling out of the sky and the death race by default.

It was the best plan he could muster under the circumstances.

"I'm at the make-it-or-break-it line, Striker. Wish me luck," Grimaldi transmitted.

A burst of static was his reply.

The missiles were in his thirty-yard range. It was now or never.

THE EXECUTIONER DIVED back into the limo the instant that his grenade detonated in the rotors. He pulled the door closed behind him and hugged the floorboards as the helicopter fell straight to the dirt and exploded. The blast front rolled over the limousine with pure seismic bedlam.

The Lincoln rocked violently, and the armored body was pelted with shrapnel. Globs of burning fuel dolloped the roof and side of the car that faced the downed chopper. Bolan knew only moments remained before the flames detonated the fuel in the gas tank.

He shrugged into the assault vest and pulled out a magazine for the M-16, palming it into the magazine well. He popped the breech on the M-203, let the smoking casing drop to the floor and thumbed in another HE bomb to replace it.

The senator got up off the carpet on his hands and knees, trying to regain his senses. Bolan went to his side and pulled him to a seated position.

"We're not clear yet. The car's burning and will blow any minute. Do you understand?"

The senator nodded groggily.

"How's Anthony?"

In answer, a groan came from the driver's compartment. Bolan leaned over the transom. James slumped over the armrest, shaking. A lot of blood splattered the dash and steering wheel. The soldier carefully checked the Secret Service agent, probing for the extent of his wounds. It didn't take him long to find it. He just followed the blood flow to the source.

Fingering the area, Bolan immediately knew that the angels were riding with this guy today. The 20 mm projectile had passed through the crook of his right arm, between the arm and the ribs, taking a chunk of bicep and latissimus dorsi with it. It could have been much worse. An inch higher and the round would have splattered the ball joint of his arm, blowing his shoulder to pieces. He'd have lost the arm and bled to death, as well.

"I think he'll make it. Give me a hand with him."

Bolan moved to one side to allow the senator to lean over the transom next to him.

"You take his left arm. I've got his wounded side."

Together, they heaved James out of the smoking driver's compartment and laid him out on his back on the rear deck.

"He's bleeding a lot," Mannix observed.

Bolan nodded. "It looks worse than it is. He'll make it."

The Executioner booted the door open opposite the burning side of the car, then threw his weapons case and duffel away from the smoking wreck. He slung the M-16/M-203 across his back, stepped out and reached back in to grab the wounded agent under the arms.

"Take his legs, John. We're going straight out, at least seventy yards. Got it?"

Mannix nodded.

Together, they did a good Airborne shuffle across the parched earth, putting a safe distance between them and the car. They placed the stricken agent on his back, then Bolan removed a field med-pack from his vest and handed it to Mannix.

"Get a compress on him."

Bolan was on his feet again and running back to retrieve his equipment. He snatched a bag up in each fist and sprinted back the way he'd come. The car exploded behind him at the fifty-yard mark, and the shock wave hit him in the back like a sonic steam-roller. He let the bags go as he was thrown forward. He tucked and rolled, landed on his back. The breath was knocked out of him, and the rifle slung across his back made the touchdown painful. He let the atmosphere clear of zinging car parts before getting back on his feet. He retrieved his bags and finished the run back to his two comrades. He dropped next to them, set the rifle on the ground next to him, then reached into the weapons case.

He pulled out a huge silver handgun holstered to black military webbing.

Bolan had the original thunder gun with him on this outing. He'd had to abandon the Desert Eagle on a recent fire mission and hadn't replaced the weapon yet. He pulled the hulking .44 AutoMag from its leather sheath and handed the weapon to Mannix.

"Know how to use one of these?"

"I was buck hunting with Lee Jurras with one of those back about when Christ was a corporal. Hell of a goddamned recoil, if I recall."

"Don't lock your elbows when you fire this."

"Oh, hell no."

Bolan grabbed the M-16 and held it at the ready. In the distance, closing, were the two squads of black-clad killers, advancing at a dead run in a straight-line front. The buttstocks of their MP-5s were extended and pressed into their firing shoulders, cheeks welded to the weapons and eyes open over the sighting blades, scanning for engageable targets.

Bolan knew that two things needed to happen very quickly: the three of them and Grimaldi needed an immediate extraction, and he needed to keep them all alive long enough so that there would be someone *to* extract. He pulled the small satellite phone out of a zippered pocket in his flight suit, activated the functions menu, scrolled to the entry "911" and hit the send button. The phone then bounced a message off a classified military communications satellite and back down to Stony Man Farm in the Blue Ridge Mountains. The message received was two words: "Defcon Five," which directed the Stony Man Farm techs to triangulate on the telemetry chip and send reinforcements ASAP.

Bolan had a subcutaneous telemetry microchip injected beneath the skin of his left shoulder for just such an occasion. It broadcast a constant RF signal that a tactical global positioning satellite could detect. Once the satellite had been instructed to search for a particular chip's signal, it would triangulate and give an exact ten-digit grid coordinate of the signal's location, accurate to ten yards. This practice had come into the vogue during the Gulf War where entire infantry platoons were injected with the chips to allow strategic leadership real-time insight into troop formations and movements as they occurred.

Once Bolan's signal was identified and pinpointed, Aaron Kurtzman could go to work coordinating the closest rapid-response assets.

Once Bolan had confirmation that the signal had been received, he left the phone with Mannix, got to his feet and went to meet the enemy head-on.

Two dozen highly trained killers against one Executioner.

Even money, sure.

3

At first, the rain started to come down in big, widely spaced drops. In five minutes, the Texas-size drizzle became a cloudburst. Little streams were quickly appearing from high-ground runoff, and the road and gravel shoulders were becoming saturated. Visibility plummeted. From inside the Gumps' Bravada, it appeared as if the atmosphere had become water. The wipers gallantly swiped away on the high setting, but the water was coming down too fast, too hard. It was like trying to drive while looking through an aquarium.

Homer Gump couldn't believe it.

He was moments away from getting the goods on the international Communist conspiracy with a digital camera and now, with all this rain, he'd be lucky to get a picture of a big black blob hovering in gray soup. Not exactly the ironclad proof that, ten minutes ago, he thought he had in the bag.

Lillian was getting shrill. "Homer, slow down! You can't even see the road in this!"

"They're going to get away, Lillian! We have to get a picture of this!"

Gump, with his face nearly pressed against the windshield, could almost see that the road was curving to the right, into a large, bowl-shaped piece of ground bordered on two sides by tabletop mesas. The heavy downpour gave way to a steady shower, and he saw the fires first, recognizing big burning shapes before his brain could catalog what the objects might have been prior to being blown to hell by some unimaginable force.

Focusing singly on getting the picture, he had failed to properly think the situation through, and he was possibly sentencing himself and his family to sure death now due to his oversight. These New World Order strike choppers were secret because somebody wanted it that way. It wouldn't be the least beneath these people to erase the Gump family right off the surface of the earth rather than to let several witnesses and a photograph of the helicopters escape containment.

With creeping dread, Gump realized that whatever had taken place here wasn't yet over.

Moving through the scrub oak and sage toward the two burning skeletons of twisted metal were ten or more black-clad man forms, running in a strangely synchronized, mechanical-looking battle drill. Gump had been exposed regularly enough to infantry doctrine and tactics to immediately grasp what those troops were trying to do out there. The elements moved in a leapfrog pattern. While half of the assault force was up and running to the next covered position, the other half was prone behind cover, laying down suppressive fire on the target. Then the process was reversed, and it would continue until the assault element overran and held fast on the far side of the objective.

Whoever was holding the high ground was making devastatingly grim use of the battlefield advantage. When the attackers decided about one-quarter of their force, five guys, would sweep in an arch to flank the large outcropping, the defender counterstruck decisively. Gump saw an incandescent muzzle-flash from the top of the rocks, dimmed in the falling rain, and three heartbeats later some kind of antipersonnel round exploded in the air just above the heads of the maneuvering fire team. Those troops were shredded from the battle helmets down and blown straight into the mud.

Scratch five enemy in one play.

He looked at his wife in the aftermath of watching five men die violently. She was goggle-eyed and gulping for air as if she were suffocating under the images of death.

Gump did the only decent thing he could. He pulled her away from the horrors of war and put her face in his shoulder. In the back seat, the kids were whimpering.

He didn't have any words of reassurance.

THE EXECUTIONER USED the sudden change of weather to his advantage.

The large outcropping had caught his eye while extracting agent James to safety with the senator. When the two dozen shock troops attacked, Bolan seized the high ground. He sprinted to the rocks, exchanging rounds with the enemy every time he gained cover. The enemy's MP-5s weren't long-range weapons, so Bolan made it into the rocks without being hit.

The rain began to fall slowly at first, then quickly picked up momentum. The downpour masked the minimal sounds he made as he climbed to the top of the rocks. From his elevated roost, the Executioner studied the enemy. The troops had fifty yards of no-man's-land to traverse before attaining a foothold at the bottom of the rocks. Let them get in a little closer, and even with the rain and open sights, the soldier knew he could make the shots.

While Bolan had no intel on the enemy, he knew he was witnessing the hidden reich's elite commando corps in action, the dreaded Werwolf units resurrected from the ashes of Nazi Germany. He immediately noted the distinctive Nazi-style black battle helmets, similar to the American Army's K-pots, but more blatantly reich inspired.

The soldiers were superbly disciplined and skilled. They maintained squad-fire-team integrity as the fire teams took turns running and covering one another. Each team moved with a fluidity and a demonstration of "group mind" that was almost spooky. When the time came for a fire team to leapfrog forward, the five soldiers, separated by twenty-five yard intervals and often out of sight of one another, popped to their feet and ran as one. As soon as the fire team in motion hit the mud, returning fire, the trailing fire team burst from cover and sprinted to the next covered position. It was a display of uncanny synchronization.

The four fire teams ate up twenty yards very rapidly. Bolan noticed one of the soldiers trailing the maneuver elements. This guy seemed more preoccupied with monitoring where his troops were and giving instructions to the soldiers via tac radio than helping lay down a base of fire. This guy would be target number one. He was in command, and taking him out could only add to the confusion of the battlefield.

Bolan raised the M-16 hybrid and peered through the rear aperture peephole and aligned it center mass with the front sight post. He placed the front sight post on the target and held the sight picture while he used the feel of the wind and the rain on his exposed skin, as well as the direction it came from, as the raw data for his sniper's mind to estimate corrections for wind velocity and bullet drop. He adjusted the sight picture up and to the left of his target. He exhaled and squeezed the trigger three times from inside that natural pause of breath.

Downrange, round number one blew a fist-size chunk of flesh and cartilage out of the guy's neck, and rounds two and three struck both sides of the collarbone. The target dropped to the ground. The assault force was now without a central leader.

Bolan had to assume that the team leaders had been designated in a descending order to take over the mission in the event that the commander was killed.

The absence of the commander didn't seem to make much of a difference.

The Executioner began taking them down as targets of opportunity presented themselves. Every time the enemy made a rush forward, he took one of them out. After losing five in a row, the enemy stayed low and concentrated on pinning down Bolan with suppressive fires. Rounds whined in disturbingly close. When rock chips from a near miss stung his cheek, he ducked and let them chew up the air above his head.

Bolan focused on the sound of the enemy's weapons fire, wondering if the "one mind, one team" trick weren't also looped into their weapons handling, as well. If these guys were as "linked" as they seemed to be, then perhaps the group would also fire their weapons as a team, each troop roughly firing when the others did, each maintaining roughly the same rate and volume of fire and each consuming ammunition at roughly the same tempo—which would mean that all of them would be changing magazines at roughly the same time.

If Bolan shifted his position and waited for that lull in fire, he could probably drop two bombs right over the top of them before they figured out his new firing niche.

The Executioner duck-walked around the rocks to occupy a new sniper position. The enemy was still concentrating their fire on the area of the rocks Bolan had just abandoned. The rain was still coming down hard, but was slowing considerably. He still had an excellent overwatch of the kill zone for the ranges he needed.

The lull in fire came as suspected. The Executioner made a mental note of this. It was something he could use against them. Two or three guys down there still had ammo, and their weapons continued to fire up at the rocks, covering the rest of the gunners, who were changing magazines. Bolan sprang into action. He got to one knee, exposing himself long enough to sight and fire the M-203. At the same instant, from down in the middle of the kill zone, there was a whoosh of solid rocket fuel being ignited. Almost simultaneous with the rocket motor roaring to life, the area of the rocks Bolan had moved erupted. The airburst HE round popped down there as Bolan hit the deck and was showered with steaming hot rubble from the rocket's impact. The Executioner was rewarded with several screams of mortal agony from down in no-man's-land. He cycled the breech of the M-203 and ejected the shell casing. By touch, he snatched another HE round off his vest and loaded it.

Bolan was up and moving again. He backed out of his position and drifted farther along on a course that would bring him down out of the rocks and into open battle.

Bolan heard yelling from the enemy ranks—one guy barking orders—and the soldier paused to eavesdrop on the instructions. The distance, the rain and the ringing in his ears from the missile exploding nearby prevented Bolan from recognizing anything the man was saying, but he knew that the words were German.

Bolan risked a look to see what they were doing.

The first five surviving troops to the far flank of the enemy line had jumped to their feet and were running like supermen around that side of the rocks, obviously dispatched to confirm Bolan's dead body or kill him if he was still alive. The troops were abandoning tactics for lightning speed. The five of them were bunching up, all of them within the kill-or-maim radius of one of Bolan's special little jewels: this 40 mm HE round was Stony Man modified to improve the Army-issue bomb's kill radius from five to twenty-five-plus yards.

Too bad for them.

Bolan raised the M-16/M-203 combo on a low arc and let the bomb fly.

He stayed low and watched the results of his lead estimation on the running targets. The five guys ran right into it. The HE shell blew up two yards above them and rained Hell onto them. Those neat Nazi-looking battle helmets protected the heads of the shock troops from being caved in by the concussion but did nothing for the rest of their bodies. The physics involved in the one-second event were tremendous. Rending magnitudes of force were released when that 40 mm warhead detonated in the space directly above the enemy.

''Canceled out'' was a mild way to describe a human body being simultaneously crushed into the dirt and blown to pieces.

Bolan became aware of something in his far visual field, back on the blacktop. It was a vehicle, stopped dead in the road and idling. A small river of water rushed between the tires. He recognized the vehicle as being the same big green SUV that had almost driven right over the top of the senator's limo.

He didn't have a clue as to why the driver decided to turn and come back this way, but the civilian presence now changed everything.

Bolan couldn't allow his warfare to touch innocents.

THE BETA TEAM PILOT rested the LCD green cross-hairs on the smoldering wreck of the Apache that lay on top of the mesa. The proximity-armed air-to-air missiles had detonated under the boom to the tail rotor. Both rocket pods were live, and the pilot directed three more of the whistlers center mass of the wreckage. The rest of the Apache disintegrated in a firestorm. On-board sensors triggered an alarm. The pilot switched from targeting to readouts. A human target was running toward the front lip of the mesa, seventy-two yards ahead.

The Apache pilot had managed to survive and bail out.

No sweat. That guy had nowhere to run or nowhere to hide from the Vulcan miniguns.

The tac-radio headset in his helmet crackled to life.

"Beta leader! Beta leader! How copy!"

It was C and C.

"Beta leader, over."

There was a surprised pause.

"What is Alpha leader's situation?"

"Unknown. The target's vehicle had an Apache gunship escort. I broke contact with the objective to pursue and finish off the gunship."

"Why wasn't this reported to me!"

"Alpha and I did our own threat assessment. We already knew what your orders would be—exactly the actions Alpha and I took. Sir, we took the initiative. Over."

"You fucking arrogant flyboys! You think you know my style? Get your ass back to the objective! Now! The Alpha leader is down! You screwups! Get the cargo, and I won't shoot you myself for this! How copy?''

''Sir, the pilot of the Apache survived the crash and is escaping.''

''Fuck their pilot! Worry about loose ends after you get the cargo!''

''Roger. Out.''

The black AeroDeth shot forward over the wreckage of the Apache, cannon armed. If the Apache's pilot presented himself as a target of opportunity, the Beta Team ace was going to take out the unlucky bastard.

JACK GRIMALDI RAN faster through the mist and rain, leaping over low sage and zigzagging around large rocks. He didn't bother to look behind him. He knew that the weird black flying tarantula of death was back there. He heard the soft whump-whump of the chopper's main rotors, a sound that was almost quiet enough to be masked by the wind and falling rain. There was the crack and hiss of missiles being fired, followed by the thumping detonations that finished off what was left of the Apache.

He poured on more speed born of desperation.

He was armed with an Ingram MAC-10 submachine gun and had spare magazines in ammo pouches clipped onto his survival vest. The weight of the little burper in his hand was no reassurance against the armored firepower of the strange black helicopter that was as silent as a soft summer breeze blowing through the trees. He wouldn't have a hope in hell of standing up to that gunship with the Ingram. He needed some heavy cover, someplace to hunker down and hide, and he needed it fast, before that hunter-killer picked up his running form on infrared and motion scans, transferred the data to targeting and quickly ended his sprint for survival.

The soft slicing of the air behind him became more furious, and the whine of the engines stepped up several notches—the bird was going into a low-level strafing run. Grimaldi was targeted. His time had run out.

He ran up the lip of the mesa and didn't even pause to see what kind of drop he was about to take. Dying in the fall would be much preferable to being blown to bits by that Vulcan. At least, if he died in a fall, there would be something left to bury in a casket. Jack Grimaldi didn't want to be buried in a sandwich bag.

The chain gun cut loose on him as his head and shoulders disappeared below the edge of the mesa. Hot, streaking green tracer rounds filled the sky overhead and raindrops sizzled in the phosphorous wake. Grimaldi hit the slick slope with both feet and slammed backward on his rear end. He slid through gravel, over rocks, sage and cactus. Then smoking 20 mm casings were raining on him as the chopper roared into the open sky and dived into the little canyon, banking to return to the scene of the ambush.

Grimaldi used his hand and weapon as impromptu brakes and bumped to a halt with his boot heels against a large rock.

He touched his throat mike.

"Striker, this is Mother Goose. Heads up, you've got incoming, buddy."

MANNIX WAS BUSY buckling the military web belt around his waist and tying the black flap-top holster to his thigh. He wiped the rain out of his eyes. He was soaked and getting just a little angry. Agent James lay on the ground near him, covered with the senator's cowhide blazer. The compress was in place, and the secret service agent was coherent. And like most dedicated agents, his mind wasn't on his own safety, but that of the senator.

"Senator, listen to me. You've got to get out of here. Commandeer that vehicle on the road, have them get you the hell out of here. I'll be okay, sir. Think about yourself, not me."

"Oh, I'm thinking about all of us, son. The whole damned family of mankind is in for a world of shit if these bastards get us today. Don't worry about me, Anthony. I'm a damned good shot."

"Senator, please!"

"Oh, save your energy for gritting your teeth when those doctors get hold of you with their alcohol pads and sutures. Your loyalty to me is awe-inspiring, son. And believe me, if we get out of this in one piece, I'm putting you in for a medal or citation. Something that will shine on your record."

James coughed, and the spasms sent lances of red-hot pain radiating from his wounded side, which popped like flashbulbs in his brain.

"Son, working yourself up is just going to work yourself over. Save it for the doctors."

"My record isn't going to look too good if you get yourself shot."

Mannix hefted the .44 AutoMag, slick and shiny with moisture, and checked the load. Eight rounds were in the magazine and one in the pipe. He had five spares in ammo pouches fastened to the black web belt. Time to shoot some rats.

"I don't think they're here to kill me. If they were, they'd have turned that limousine into scrap metal from the get-go, don't you think?"

James didn't respond to that analysis. He just frowned. Uprange, the enemy small-arms fire continued furiously, but the enemy was no longer advancing. They were holding covered positions and waiting for Pollock to offer them a target of opportunity. The gutsy bastard had already thinned their ranks by almost half, and whoever was left in charge up there was thinking twice about continuing with the suicide charge.

Mannix pulled down the leather blazer thrown over James, reached under the man's suit coat and unfastened the mini-Uzi from the shoulder rig. He covered the agent with the blazer and put the Uzi in the man's good hand.

"Here. You might need this if they get through me."

"You take it."

"Oh, hell no. This silver hawgleg is all I'm gonna need. As your superior in this matter, I insist."

Reluctantly, James took the mini-Uzi from the senator.

"Good luck, Senator."

"And godspeed to you, son."

Mannix gave James a reassuring squeeze on his good shoulder and moved out. The land sloped gently upward from his position, getting steeper near the rock face Pollock was using as a fortress. Mannix wondered how the colonel might attack this problem as he threaded his way toward where he figured he'd launch his attack. He stayed low, crouch-walking through brush to stay out of sight. He worked his way downslope in a wide arc before moving back up toward the rocks. He was maneuvering himself behind the enemy, intending to catch them off guard while their attention was focused on those rocks.

While he wasn't a trained soldier, he was a very adept hunter. Both occupations required cunning and common sense. Mannix hadn't attained his position in life without having ample amounts of both qualities. He worked his way up a runoff gully that put him behind what was left of the black-clad troopers. Watching for the winking globes of fire from the muzzle blasts, he was able to locate where the enemy had gone to ground. He counted ten firing positions and at least two more that he couldn't see but could hear.

His closest potential target was upslope about thirty-five yards at about a one-o'clock position. The guy was hunkered into a cluster of large rocks, firing around the edge of one toward Pollock's general direction. He could see the top of the black battle helmet bobbing over the rocks intermittently but from where he was crouched, not enough of the guy was exposed to offer a really good target. Mannix would have to close on his prey to get the sight picture he wanted. He couldn't afford to fire and miss, alerting the troops to the threat from the rear without thinning their ranks at the same time.

He figured that he'd have to close the gap by half that distance to deliver a killing shot.

The snakeskin cowboy boots he wore weren't the best footwear for stealth but the prevailing weather was a good ally. He came out of the gully on all fours, crawling forward, keeping his eyes locked on the battle helmet that was his first target.

Mannix was twenty yards out, in a duck walk now, when he lost his footing on a rain-slick rock and fell on his chest with a loud thud, displacing loose gravel and stone, alerting the intended quarry.

The gunner reacted like a spring-steel rattlesnake. He flipped from his belly to his back and sat up faster than Mannix thought a man could move. Those bastards weren't normal, he thought as he rolled to his right and a hailstorm of 9 mm rounds chewed up the air and ground he'd just vacated. The MP-5 the gunner was packing stopped its stuttering fusillade abruptly; the bolt locked back on a smoking chamber while the guy was yelling to his comrades, "The rear! The rear!" in German.

The gunner's eyes tracked the senator, blue, soulless and unblinking while his hands were a blur of motion, dropping the spent magazine, replacing it with a fresh one. Those eyes gave the Texan quite a chill. Devil doll's eyes, forever locked into a hundred-yard stare, tranced out. Zombies blindly executing instructions.

Mannix came out of the roll and lay flat on his chest, arms thrust straight out, bringing the

AutoMag to bear in a two-fisted grip. He quick-sighted down the ventilated rib barrel and fired. His forearms jumped off the ground in the recoil, a yard of flame erupting from the muzzle.

The 240-grain slug connected with the enemy under the chin and blew him backward to the ground. There was no question that the guy was dead.

Mannix jumped to his feet and raced in the opposite direction. He heard a guy back there yelling, *"Schnell! Schnell!"* and the crunch-thump of multiple boot heels pounding the ground in hot pursuit. He had figured the troops weren't there to kill him until his pursuers began to fire on him, the bullets parting the rain close enough to feel the breeze. He dropped into the runoff gully and gratefully didn't crash and burn. He headed downhill, taking them away from Anthony, away from the rock face Pollock was using as a sniper's nest.

The Team assessed his mission as a success. He'd divided the enemy along two fronts, and that's how Germany had lost the big one.

In that moment, John Mannix was more alive than he'd ever been before.

WHAT THE BETA TEAM leader saw through the bubble of the AeroDeth's cockpit canopy was enough to almost make him panic. He was momentarily indecisive, wondering whether he should report this latest disaster to C and C. However, C and C was already in a blind rage over the Apache fiasco, and to not report what was taking place below would be the capper. He'd assuredly be executed on the spot for his compounding mistakes.

The precious cargo was on foot, running like hell away from the ambush, zigging and zagging quite impressively for a man his age. The pilot supposed that he could perform similarly if he had five kill-programmed Werwolf shock troops snapping at his heels with automatic weapons blazing, hot to make the shot that dropped the man they'd come to kidnap—not kill. How this glitch in their programming had taken place was anyone's guess, but the pilot had no illusions as to what was necessary to salvage the situation.

He wasn't going to take that action independently. No way. He had to have the green light first.

He broke radio silence unceremoniously.

"Sir, Beta leader. If I don't fire on our own troops now, they're about ten seconds away from putting the bag on the precious cargo. Forever."

C and C didn't ask for details.

"Open fire, goddammit! Open fire! Protect the precious cargo!"

"Roger."

The pilot really didn't feel any remorse about what he did next. It wasn't as if those troops down there were human anymore. They were more, but in all the ways that counted, those troops were far, far less. Each man's individual destiny was no longer his own.

The pilot's natural inclination was to look left when scanning a target, so that's where he started. He reflexively shifted his eyes up and to the left. The rotating barrels on the 20 mm Vulcan cannon spoke authoritatively and with indisputable finality. Target number one disappeared into an explosive chunky red mist. It was about a one-second burst, and still it was overkill. He moved his head slightly to the right and brought target number two into his green electronic crosshairs. The eyes went up and to the left. Target number two vaporized. Targets three, four and five tried to make the kill harder by running evasive patterns on the ground that were too slow, too late.

The precious cargo had hit the dirt with the first fusillade from the hovering gunship. Now he was returning fire with some kind of hand cannon. The bullet strikes against the armored skin of the aircraft sounded like jackhammer blows on a bank vault door. The pilot wasn't concerned; the armor would hold.

"Precious cargo is safe," he reported.

"Then secure the precious cargo, team leader."

"Roger."

In the distance, he noticed the forest-green Bravada for the first time, engine running, stopped dead in the middle of the highway. The driver's-side door was open, and running toward the helicopter through the moderate rainfall was a portly older man wearing a designer T-shirt, tree-bark-pattern camo pants, sneakers and a Dallas Cowboys ball cap. The guy would stop every several strides as he ran forward, pausing to raise a small box to his face before running forward again.

The lunatic was taking pictures of the helicopter.

The pilot reported the activity.

"I have an unknown civilian element on the ground taking pictures of the helicopter, sir."

C and C's response was predictable.

"No loose ends."

"Roger."

The pilot swung the helicopter around to gain a positive target lock. It was the last thing he ever did.

The 66 mm rocket struck the canopy bubble dead center. The black helicopter went nova thirty-three yards off the deck. The flaming hulk fell to the dirt in sections, the burning wreckage igniting a forty-by-twenty-yard inferno in the surrounding area that steamed in the falling rain.

The Werwolf troops in the rear never knew what hit them.

HOMER GUMP COULDN'T believe it—the second black chopper emerged out of the mist. The regal bitch of Fortune had rolled out a second chance for him to hit the big time. The visions were back, flashing before his mind's eye. The mountain of money he'd get for publication rights alone to print the damning photos in various magazines would make the Homer Gump household into a minifiefdom. Then there'd be the radio and talk shows. The highest bidder would win, of course, and he'd become a hero within the patriot-survivalist camps. He'd be invited as keynote speaker to all the patriot meetings and summits that took place dozens of times throughout any given year in these twilight days of the Republic.

Homer Gump would finally be a contender.

The black helicopter halted in the air and hovered. A man was running with all his might toward the helicopter, chased by five of the black-clad soldiers. The nose gun on the gunship roared to life, belching out ten yards of flame in a one-second burst, and one of those soldiers ceased to exist.

"Holy Jesus!"

Lillian sobbed louder.

Gump snatched the digital camera off the console and popped his door. He was losing valuable imagery. Nothing was sacred to these bastards. They'd blow up their own troops to get what they wanted. Pictures of that helicopter massacring its own people would be priceless.

"Homer! Where are you going? Don't leave us!"

Gump turned to tell Lillian to relax and when he did, the nose gun spoke again and another soldier was blown to smoky bits.

"Goddammit! I'm going to lose these pictures, Lillian!"

Gump darted into the rain and raised the camera. He started clicking away and captured the images of the rest of those soldiers being callously murdered. He wanted a really good picture of that helicopter, one showing all the detail so analysts could divine her secrets from detailed computer-enhanced studies of the image. For that, he was going to have to get a lot closer.

He didn't think twice about what that could mean. All he saw was the fame and fortune that the pictures could buy.

He ran fifty yards forward, stopped and clicked another picture. Then he was running again. The weird helicopter had to have seen him then, because the chopper did a neat little pivot in midair so that the nose gun was trained on him.

Gump froze in his tracks, realizing that his own

death was just a heartbeat away. There was no place to run, no place to hide. It would be stupid to even try. And he could hear the regal bitch of Fortune cackling with glee through the evaporated vapors of his own ambitions.

He didn't want to die looking up at that thing. He turned his back, a man who had accepted the cards being dealt. He wanted his last sight on earth to be that of his family, his wife. He knew they'd be next, then they'd all be together again soon, someplace where nobody could ever hurt them again.

He found peace in that thought and waited for it all to end.

THE EXECUTIONER DROPPED to the ground and rolled. He got to his feet and sprinted down the slope, the Beretta 93-R an extension of his right fist, the long, skinny suppressor tube screwed to the handgun's barrel. The M-16/M-203 combo was slung across his back, retired now because the job at hand required a weapon for close-in precision work. He was capitalizing on the confusion generated by the senator's unexpected attack from the rear and the return of the second unidentified military helicopter. The remaining troopers, four of them now, were too preoccupied with the plays unfolding between the gunship and their comrades in pursuit of that crazy Texan.

Bolan was going to remind them of the dangers in being distracted.

The first guy Bolan reached was lying prone, looking behind him while his buddies were being systematically brutalized downrange. The Executioner made a quiet bird call, loud enough to startle the guy into jerking around to focus on the tall, black-clad wraith standing over him. The Beretta coughed twice, and two bubbling holes popped open on the trooper's forehead. The guy was kicked onto his back and shuddered into death.

The next guy in line was in a crouch, orientating on the hovering helicopter. He'd heard the Beretta's whisper, and wet rock ground under his boots as he pivoted toward the danger too late. The Executioner rushed toward him, firing on the run. The gunner took a 9 mm bullet right through the bridge of his nose, and round number two shattered his chin.

He flopped backward and skidded away from the Executioner as Bolan jumped across the man's fighting position, angling in for kill number three.

From twenty yards, Bolan shot the guy left in command through his snarling lips as he spun to face the charging Executioner. The guy backflipped into a muddy slide, his dying nerves firing impotently and he stitched the heavens with a one-gun salute.

And then there was one.

Rocket Man found himself toting a defanged launcher tube with no time left on the clock to drop it and bring his slung MP-5 into play. He tried to and lost.

Getting that rocket launcher had been Bolan's goal since he'd leaped off the rocks and into the battlefield. He sprinted to the dead man and his rocket launcher, dropping the Beretta at his feet as he snatched the launch tube off the ground and quickly familiarized himself with the design. Like those helicopters, the launcher was of a make and manufacturer unknown to the world's arms markets. The launch tube was made out of steel and collapsed like a LAW. This launcher was reusable, not a disposable unit like the American LAW. The weapon just reeked of German practicality. Waste not, want not. Bolan liberated a 66 mm warhead from the dead commando's body and slid the projectile into the rear of the launcher. He closed and latched the firing gate, then shouldered the launch tube.

The launcher sighted in almost identically to the LAW weapons system. He targeted the cockpit canopy of the black gunship and let the missile fly. There was a sharp crack as the rocket engine ignited, and a whoosh of flame blasted out the back end as the lethal javelin left the tube. A thin trail of smoke described the warhead's trajectory as it raced across the intervening distance, accelerating as it breached the small-arms-proof Plexiglas and detonated in the pilot's face.

The helicopter blew apart in the sky. The fireball wasn't as impressive as the Executioner would have expected. The explosion of the warhead should have touched off the fuel in the tanks like a mininuke. Maybe the bird was running low on gas. The wreckage rained to the earth and created a nice little inferno nonetheless.

Bolan didn't have any more time to ponder the strange lack of burning fuel in the helicopter's demise. He dropped the launcher, retrieved the Beretta and jogged through the smoky haze that hung in the air despite the falling rain.

He found the Texas senator laying facedown in the mud, playing possum.

Mannix heard the crunch of Bolan's approaching stride and he raised his head, smiling when he saw who it was.

He said cheerily, "Well, I'm damned glad you're not having an off day today."

4

Not many people knew what his real name was.

Those of his inner circle referred to him as Joe. Joseph F. Newport. He was a no-nonsense kind of hardass, and his reputation for ruthlessness was well earned.

Newport wasn't a pleasant fellow to be around, for his superiors or for his subordinates. Especially his subordinates. Subordinates were, by definition, inferior and incompetent.

Newport didn't like the masses of humanity.

The masses were like subordinates, preferring the path of least resistance, followers eager for someone to do their thinking for them. Newport couldn't wait to have the ovens lit again, day and night burning the dead husks of the inferiors after being worked to death as slaves from inside the concentration camps that were already prepared.

He handled all sensitive operations for the Committee. Sensitive Operations—SENSOPS—under Joe Newport was the SS reborn. Right down to the requirement that all operatives for SENSOPS wear black. The fabled Men in Black were no joke; they were SENSOPS agents, and all of them packed top secret security clearances within the U.S. intelligence community, which gave them access to everything.

Any time the National Security Council met behind bug-proof doors, there in the background watching was the black specter of SENSOPS. The President, the Joint Chiefs, Congressional committees—no one in the U.S. government had a door that could be closed to SENSOPS personnel. SENSOPS monitored and manipulated the inner workings of the U.S. government in all the places that mattered.

Senator John Mannix was the wild card. His job, on paper, was to monitor the intelligence services. Mannix wasn't one of their puppets. They had people on the oversight committee, but they didn't own the committee. Since Mannix couldn't be bought or seduced to serve the dark side, he'd have to be killed or sent to "charm school." The Committee had decided against assassination. Mannix was sentenced to thirty days in charm school. Newport's job was to make sure that the senator didn't miss his first day in class.

The senator's sudden disappearance from the scene was already planned. Mannix's own press secretary was cued up and ready to go on camera to the nation that recent grave events in the country's schools had compelled the senator to go into seclusion to meditate on a legislative response to the tragedy. Strong hints would be made that the senator was in a war of conscience over his former hardline support of the Second Amendment and the gun lobby. In other words, expect the senator to start acting like a good Democrat any day now.

After thirty days in the mind-control dungeons of

Project Monarch, Mannix would return to Washington with an entirely new agenda. He would wholeheartedly support stiffer gun laws and the total banning of assault rifles for private ownership. He would favor the advantages of security over civil liberties. Overnight he would transform from a staunch civil libertarian to a law-and-order fanatic. He would vote and argue for any legislation that unleashed more cops, more guns for cops, more helicopters to spy on the population. Mannix would be working very hard after graduation to dissolve the American republican state and replace it with the global Gestapo state that the Committee had high hopes for making a reality.

But someone was monkey-wrenching Newport's perfect snatch operation. He didn't know what it was like anymore to be handed his ass in a brown paper grocery bag. He never liked how that felt. To feel as if he were out of control of a situation made him furious. He wanted to identify that someone and kill him. Make him suffer.

The Beta Team leader had acknowledged orders to tie up the loose ends.

Then…nothing. Just a sky full of static. That pilot was in too much trouble to be willfully ignoring his radio calls. The only explanation was that the pilot was no longer physically able to answer because the helicopter had been blown out of the sky. Newport could only assume that whoever the enemy was, that enemy was still alive out there and was now in possession of some very sensitive wreckage. That couldn't be allowed. It was the kind of evidence that could open a can of worms he didn't even want to contemplate.

Newport tore off the radio headset and threw it against the console. The corpsmen in the cramped compartment with him feigned engrossed interest in their own equipment.

"Goddammit!"

He shook a cigarette out of the pack he'd been carrying with him for months. Even though he'd quit, he tapped the cigarette butt to tamp the tobacco, then stuck it in his mouth. He stood and began to pace up and down the narrow aisle. The corpsmen scooted out of his way. He nibbled on the cigarette filter as he considered his options to best regain containment.

Newport wasn't so arrogant that he never planned contingencies for an operation gone awry. Even the best laid plans plotted by tactical geniuses could unravel. There had to be backup.

The standing procedure, an SOP Newport had instituted himself, was for operatives utilizing air assets to always plan for the eventuality of having to salvage the wreckage of a downed AeroDeth helicopter in the middle of a major operation. Newport knew that he could keep a lid on the fiasco even if the wreckage did fall into potentially damaging hands. With the Committee's absolute backroom power over everything that mattered from inside the U.S. national security complex, he knew that he would get the seized wreckage back somewhere in transit, when it went to depot. The U.S. military brass would give it back, with apologies over the whole mix-up. He still didn't need it to go that far.

Recapturing the damning evidence at the depot would still be read as failure on Newport's part to keep the operation discreet.

Regardless, he held all the trump cards to any situation that might develop.

The Committee paid Newport a generous salary, an executive-level paycheck, that was deposited monthly into a reich-owned bank in Munich. The paycheck that gave him so much delight was the monthly check from Uncle Sam—a compensatory token compared to the Committee's contribution to his retirement—one cut from the FEMA allocation in the federal budget. As Lance Finnig, Newport was the assistant to the director of FEMA. In the field, Newport was the director, authorized to wield the same powers, privileges and decision-making latitude that the director enjoyed, licenses that had once been consolidated exclusively in the hands of the President. During the Bush-era, through executive order, the President delegated all powers that had previously been vested to him solely by the Disaster Relief and Emergency Assistance Act of 1988 into the hands of the director of FEMA.

The Federal Emergency Management Agency was conceived by the Nixon administration and refined by Jimmy Carter's. In 1979, Congress waved the budgetary wand, and FEMA opened its doors as the newest federal kid on the block. Newspaper accounts mentioning the agency always made reference to disaster relief, and quickly that association was embedded in the public eye. The national media outlets generally never reported that FEMA's ability to relieve disasters was grossly incompetent and the agency had been booted out by the local authorities in the wake of Hurricane Hugo. FEMA was a bigger disaster than the hurricane had been.

FEMA's incompetence in providing potable water, makeshift shelter and passing out toilet paper was probably due to the fact that the agency had nothing to do with disaster relief. FEMA's legislated job was to provide continuity in government in the event of a nationally declared emergency, which in plain English meant that FEMA would take over the role and function of the federal government if the President were to ever declare a national state of emergency. FEMA would be the government for as long as the state of emergency existed. FEMA had authorization to invoke and activate every one of the President's emergency powers declared by executive order, which, in a state of declared emergency, made the agency the ad hoc government, as dictatorial as necessary to maintain order.

In a nationally declared state of emergency, martial law would be invoked and the rights and guarantees of the U.S. Constitution would go into a Smithsonian vault for safekeeping until the emergency passed. The President's emergency power to suspend the Constitution and declare martial law was now FEMA's prerogative, too. As long as a state of emergency existed, all other federal agencies—to include all branches of the military—would fall under the authority of FEMA.

It was a beautiful piece of work, this brainchild of the Committee, to bring the great Republic to its final curtain via one of its very own and authorized federal agencies.

Newport plucked the cigarette from his mouth and returned it to the pack. He pocketed the pack of cigarettes and went to the bulkhead, punching the red button on the intercom squawk box mounted at lip level.

"Driver, get back on the highway and proceed south."

"Yes, sir."

The big diesel engine turned over, then the M-111 two-and-a-half ton military truck lurched forward, stuttered and lurched again. The driver cursed his bad clutch work, knowing what it was doing to the Tactical Operations Center module riding piggyback on the truck's bed. A twin of the first truck followed it back onto the highway.

Newport went into action, scrambling his contingency assets to converge on the target. An Army reserve MP company, a heavy-equipment engineer battalion and a civil-affairs company were conducting maneuvers in the surrounding countryside. Standing by in Big Spring was a FEMA hazardous-material team.

By satellite phone, Newport contacted the director and asked for full operational authority to shut down west Texas, if necessary.

"Loyalty is honor," the director said.

"Yes, and the mighty shall inherit the earth," Newport replied.

The sequence was completed whereby two strangers might come to know that they were brothers.

"You have called to report a successful wrap-up to your mission."

"No. There have been a few complications. I need full operational authority for west Texas."

"Complications, my friend?"

"The target has introduced an unknown set of variables into the matrix. Both of our air assets are down. I have to achieve containment and begin salvage operations. I need full operational authority for west Texas. Now, sir."

"You have it."

"Thank you. Everything will be in my report."

"I'm confident that it will."

Newport broke the connection and smiled. Now all he had to do was cordon off the area and take the quarry right out in the open in front of God and everybody.

The ability to do that and get away with it—now, that was real power.

Stony Man Farm, Virginia

UPON RECEIPT of the satellite transmission from Mack Bolan, Aaron "the Bear" Kurtzman went to work at his terminal. He patched into the global positioning satellite network and scanned for Bolan's chip signal. He found the signal in west Texas, close to Big Spring. A separate window popped open on the computer monitor, and Bolan's vitals were displayed. Well, the guy was still alive. From the looks of those readouts, the Executioner was getting an exciting workout.

Kurtzman opened a phone line via modem and had the computer dial a number in the Justice Department. It was the red-line number, reserved exclusively for communications between Stony Man Farm and Hal Brognola.

Kurtzman bypassed the usual pleasantries. "I just received a Defcon Five from Striker. He's in west Texas, just outside of Big Spring." He gave the big Fed the ten-digit grid and map directions.

Brognola read the information back.

"That's the gist of it," Kurtzman stated.

"I'll take care of it," Brognola said, and broke the connection.

Texas

THE FEMA CONVOY PULLED onto the shoulder just outside the containment area to link up with the hazmat team. Newport got up front in the cab of the truck before ordering the convoy back on the road. The sun through the breaking storm clouds was dipping low in the west, and Newport wanted to be fully in control before the sun set. At least the salvage operation was going to have the benefit of cover of darkness. By morning, the containment area would be sterilized and the compromising wreckage crated and in transit to their secret location inside Area 51, Groom Lake, Nevada.

Two hundred yards up the road from the crash site, the convoy encountered a cordon of three Texas State Police cars, blocking both lanes of traffic. One trooper was out front, waving his hands above his head. The lead truck braked and the convoy came to a halt.

Newport climbed out of the cab and confronted the trooper.

"Trooper, as of 1643 hours, FEMA is officially in charge of this operation."

"Could I see some identification, sir?"

Newport snatched his ID wallet out of his suit coat and handed it to the trooper without opening it.

"Thank you, sir."

The trooper opened the wallet and studied the badge and ID. He flicked the wallet shut and handed it back.

"Sir, we have received no information on FEMA taking charge of this crime scene."

"Now you have."

"Sir, I have to confirm this with Colonel Pollock."

"Who?"

"Colonel Pollock is in charge of this situation. He's acting under presidential authority, and we have that confirmed by the Justice Department."

"Trooper, I think you better inform Colonel Pollock that he has been relieved of command. I'm in charge now."

JACK GRIMALDI TORE away the smoking engine cowl and peered into the steamy interior. The wreckage of the second black helicopter was still hot and he was wearing a pair of Army-issue leather work gloves to protect his hands.

Grimaldi paled at what he saw.

A metal sphere was inside the compartment, held in place by steel bracing. The sphere was hooked into the rest of the helicopter's mechanical and power systems via wires and hoses. It was the decal on the surface of the sphere that caused Grimaldi's blood to run cold: the red-and-yellow universal symbol for a radiation hazard.

That sphere, no larger than a beach ball, was a nuclear generator.

Grimaldi jumped off the smoking fuselage and backed away fifty yards.

"Colonel! I think you better have a look at this!"

Bolan looked up from the conversation he was having with the ranking state trooper on the scene. Grimaldi was up the rise, yelling and waving his hands to get his attention.

The Executioner trotted up the rise and joined his old friend.

"Problem, Jack? Did you find something?"

"Yeah, I think I found something, Sarge. I found out why there was no fireball from the fuel tanks going up."

"And?"

"There *are* no fuel tanks. That bird is nuclear powered."

"What?"

"Yeah, and it's the damnedest thing I've ever seen. I didn't know they could make nuclear power plants that small. If it's one of ours, it's so damned classified that nobody outside of Groom Lake would even have knowledge of this project. It might be interesting to see who comes to claim the wreckage."

Bolan just nodded. He was feeling a little cold inside, thinking about the kind of resources his enemy had access to. They not only had resources, but they also had power. They could field aircraft, ordnance and technology that the rest of the world was largely unaware of. It would have been unbelievable if it wasn't for the evidence of his own senses and the bloody ordeal of the past hour.

"It probably wouldn't be a bad idea to call in some kind of hazmat," Grimaldi added.

"I'm on it."

"It's a good thing you didn't shoot the engine with that rocket."

"Yeah, I hear you."

"Sarge, what the hell is going on here?"

THE STATE TROOPER in charge of the roadblock yelled, "All right! Let these vehicles through! Let these vehicles through!"

Two troopers jumped behind the wheels of their cruisers. The powerful V-8 interceptor engines roared to life, and the cruisers reversed out of the way onto the shoulder. Joe Newport didn't bother to get back in the cab. He hopped up on the running board, held on to the mirror and said, "Drive."

The FEMA convoy jolted forward in stutters before smoothing out and rolling into the containment area. Newport jumped to the pavement as the truck braked with hydraulic pops and hisses. He put his hands on his hips and critically surveyed his playing field.

There was a disco show of emergency lights from the ten state patrol cars and two paramedic ambulances parked along both sides of the highway in skewered, conflicting angles. Several state troopers were attempting to get the respective fires under control with small extinguishers. Two troopers were getting a statement from a portly civilian standing next to a big green monstrosity of a vehicle. That had to be the guy with the camera. Newport memorized the license-plate number for future reference. Another group of troopers huddled around a man on the ground being attended by paramedics. The senator was among the group, and the two locked eyes across the spanning distance.

The senator laughed loudly and broke away from the crowd, jogging toward the FEMA man. Newport eyed the web belt and the huge handgun holstered and tied to the senator's thigh. Mannix had his gun hand on the butt of the weapon like Marshal Dillon drawing down on the black-hat drifter in the middle of the town square at high noon.

Newport pulled the pack of cigarettes from his shirt pocket and snapped out the same cigarette. He pocketed the cigarette pack and flipped the unlit cigarette across his knuckles before putting it between his lips. He watched the big Texan as he negotiated the fifty yards of desert to the roadside.

Newport's greeting was curt. "Senator."

Mannix kept his hand on the butt of the AutoMag.

"Mr. Finnig, your response time is too good to believe. It makes me think you were out there in the desert all along waiting to move in."

"You can believe as you wish, Senator. I'm in charge now. Where is this Colonel Pollock?"

Men in protective gear were jumping off the hazmat truck at the tail of the convoy, moving out at a double time toward the downed chopper, brandishing Geiger counters.

Mannix watched them fan out before addressing

Newport again. "Is there some kind of environmental hazard here, Mr. Finnig?"

"As a matter of fact, yes, there is. A radioactive one."

JACK GRIMALDI WHISTLED.

"Presto requesto, we have hazmat."

"Yeah, hazmat that I haven't even requested yet."

"Maybe they're here to stake a claim on their property."

"It's not their property anymore."

The two Stony Man warriors ran down the rise. The state-police lieutenant intercepted them near the road. Bolan and Grimaldi didn't stop for the trooper; he had to jog along with them.

"Colonel, I have just been informed by state headquarters that Mr. Lance Finnig of FEMA is now in charge of this salvage operation. I'm sorry, sir."

"Like hell he is," Bolan said.

"This is straight from Washington, Colonel."

"I have presidential authority in this matter, Lieutenant."

"So do they, sir."

The Oval Office,
Washington, D.C.

THE PRESIDENT HAD CLEARED his calendar for the day and was looking forward to some quiet time alone, just the chief executive in his office doing paperwork. Before he could pick up the files and sort through them, the door opened and the vice president burst in with the director of FEMA in tow.

The Man could think of many people he would have rather seen barge unannounced into his inner sanctum than those two particular men. He didn't like his second in command. The President had been told that if he wanted to ever see the inside of the Oval Office from behind the desk of the commander in chief, he'd take Trent Moore as his running mate. Since he really did want to see the inside of the Oval Office from behind that desk, he rationalized Trent Moore as the price he had to pay to win the presidency.

Moore always looked ready for the country club or a photo opportunity. His raven-black hair was Ivy League and aggressively moussed with young Turk machismo. He wore a navy-blue blazer, red silk tie and sky-blue Oxford cloth shirt that were impeccably tailored to his lean, handball player's physique. Moore was more than just another punk political opportunist; he was a punk political opportunist on a fanatic's crusade. The guy had written several alarmist, reactionary tracts on the impending ecological Armageddon if Western development wasn't stopped dead in its tracks. He was at the forefront of every new UN treaty that had anything to do with the environment or biological diversity.

The President suspected that's why they liked Trent Moore and wanted him in the vice president's office. He knew that the Nazi operatives in the government were aiming to unleash the global reich through the United Nations system. He knew that before the UN could become a de facto world state, the UN would have to be given power over its subject members. Every one of those environmental and biological diversity-based treaties with the UN were quickly piling up and giving the United Nations jurisdiction over every clump of dirt on the land or beneath the sea.

What was even clearer now to the President was that they never cared who got into the White House in the first place, as long as Trent Moore went into the deal as vice president. Moore was COMCON's boy, and if he was ever elected President, all they needed was the first ten minutes on the clock from the time Moore was sworn into office. Moore could make the declaration of the national emergency right on the White House lawn, and then FEMA would take over the government under invocation of martial law. The era of the American Republic would be over.

The President knew the law read that FEMA couldn't stand in for the federal government for a period of more than five years. Five years was a long time, and the President knew that they wouldn't waste any time about declaring the UN a fully operative world state and announce the advent of the thousand-year reign of the world reich. The world's populations would be divided into two groups: desirables and undesirables. The undesirables would be hauled off to slave camps and worked to death or killed outright. The stench of burning human flesh would rise up from foul chimneys all over the globe. The slaughter would begin anew, on a scale that staggered anything accomplished by Hitler and the Third Reich.

Things weren't looking good for the home team.

"This better be important, Trent," the President said. "I was hoping to have some quiet time right now."

"Quiet time's going to have to go on hold."

The President looked at the director of FEMA. "You're not declaring the national emergency ahead of schedule, are you? Before you get the chance to run me out of office and install your good little yes man here?"

Moore visibly colored but didn't say anything.

The director of FEMA chuckled.

"No, Mr. President. I'm here to inform you that a situation has developed in west Texas and that my agency is taking over jurisdiction in west Texas."

"I appreciate your having the courtesy to let me know this."

"I believe in being decent about it. We have a problem in west Texas, and I need to call in a favor."

"I didn't think I owed you a favor."

"You owe them that desk you're sitting behind," the vice president said with a sneer.

The President stared down his insubordinate second in command, then shifted his gaze back to the director of FEMA.

"What could I possibly help you with?"

The director returned the flint-edged eyeballing the President was giving him.

"Apparently you have an operative working on your authority in the containment area who refuses to recognize our seizure of jurisdiction in this matter. This man of yours seems ready to defend his claim to jurisdiction with deadly force. I need you to pick up that phone and tell this guy he's been overruled.''

The President didn't reach for the phone.

"Or?"

The director slammed both palms on the desk and leaned his scarlet-hued face over the desktop.

"Or I'll make a phone call and send a team of jocks up to that school—Princeton, isn't it?—to party with that prissy daughter of yours. I'll make sure they take all night and send you a copy of it on video!''

The President jumped to his feet and knotted his fists into the other man's lapels. He was shaking with rage and fear. He knew the sick bastards would do it.

"You stay away from my daughter, you son of a bitch! Do you understand me?''

The director picked up the phone. "Then make that phone call.''

The President made the phone call.

Texas

JOE NEWPORT TURNED to face his opponent for the first time. The man was big; six-foot-plus and at least two hundred pounds. He was wearing a black flight suit, combat boots and an assault vest heavy with ammunition and ordnance. An M-16/M-203 rifle combo was slung muzzle down across the man's back. There was no doubt that this man was a professional soldier.

The man walking beside the black-clad soldier could only be the Apache's pilot.

"Colonel Pollock, I presume."

Cold blue eyes were scanning him like an X-ray beam.

"Who are you?"

"I'm taking over from here. That's all you need to know."

"Like hell you are."

"Like hell I am. I have all the authority I need. If your name really is Pollock and you really do work with the Justice Department, then you fall under me in the chain of command, soldier. Maybe the senator here can explain the letter of the law in this case to you better than I can."

Newport locked eyes with the Texan. "Senator?"

Mannix squirmed, knowing that the man was right.

"Well, assuming that an emergency has been declared—"

"It has been," Newport replied. "FEMA is running west Texas right now."

Bolan looked at Mannix. "This guy's with FEMA?"

"This guy, Colonel, is Assistant Director Lance Finnig of FEMA."

Bolan looked back at Newport.

"This is a damned long way from Washington, Finnig."

"And you're just a boot in the ass away from landing in the stockade, soldier."

The silence was deadly for several heartbeats.

"Only the President can tell me to break off."

"The President? I guess you want this done by the book, have the President himself tell you what is and what isn't, is that it? Got to get it straight from the Gipper, huh, boy? Okay, I'll play ball. I'll show you I can get your President to tell you to break off. You just cool your boot heels, soldier boy."

Newport stepped out of earshot and had a short conversation into his cell phone.

The director was already in the White House, there to announce FEMA's activation in west Texas. Newport instructed the director to do whatever he had to do to get the President to call off his attack dog and put a muzzle on him.

Then Newport went back toe-to-toe with Bolan.

He said in low tones, "You're about to discover that you're living in a world that doesn't exist anymore at the top of the food chain. In our New World Order, soldier boy, you'll be a dinosaur. An enemy of the state."

Newport gestured toward the carnage in the background.

"Your skill impresses me, I must admit. There still might be a place for you in—"

"There will never be a place for me in your world, pal."

The Executioner's voice was as cold as a November graveyard. The hostility washing off Bolan backed Newport up a step or two.

He regained his composure with a taunting laugh. "Then I guess your inability to adapt will mark you for extinction. Maybe not today." He frowned. "With all these cops snooping around and all.

Maybe not tomorrow. But the day will come, Mr. Patriot, when you will have no choice but to acknowledge that we are in control now.''

"That won't be any day soon."

"You think you can stop the future, soldier boy? History has decreed that we are the future."

"There's still a lot of history left in this country."

Newport laughed contemptuously. "Okay, you go right on thinking that. But it won't be healthy when you finally have to face reality."

Mannix broke the standoff with a yelp. Something was humming in his pocket like a vibrator. It was that high-speed cell phone he'd immediately pocketed after Bolan had tossed it to him. The senator pulled the vibrating phone out of his pocket and offered it to Bolan.

"That's for you," Newport said. "I know."

The Executioner took the phone.

"Striker."

Bolan recognized the voice immediately. It was the Man.

"Striker, as your commander in chief, I'm ordering you to surrender jurisdiction to FEMA. FEMA has overriding authority in this matter. Is that understood?"

The Executioner didn't answer for a heartbeat. There was something he had to know.

"Sir, are you one of them?"

"Son, sometimes the bear gets you, sometimes you get the bear. Do you understand?"

The Executioner understood perfectly.

Bolan said, "Yes, sir" and broke the connection.

Keeping his eyes on Newport, he called over his shoulder to the state-police lieutenant.

"Lieutenant, come here, please!"

The state trooper joined the two men warily. He'd overheard some of the heated words exchanged between the two Feds, and he didn't like what he was hearing. But he had his orders.

"Colonel."

"Lieutenant, I want Jack, the senator and his wounded man loaded into one of those ambulances. I want two of your cruisers out in front of the ambulance. I want that civilian family following the ambulance. I'll be riding with you in your car, and I want a couple more of your cars behind us. We're going to the hospital. When we get to the hospital, I want every man you can field to set up a perimeter around the hospital, and you will hold that perimeter until relieved in place. Do you understand the instructions, Lieutenant?"

The trooper gulped and looked to Newport for guidance.

The man shrugged.

"Yes, Colonel."

"Then move it, Trooper!"

The trooper bolted away and began to yell for his men to fall in.

The Executioner took a step into Newport's personal space so the guy could see the cold Reaper in his eyes.

"Don't interfere with our evac. I'll shoot you dead if you do."

"You've got a white flag, soldier boy. Take it."

"On my oath as a United States soldier, I'm duty

bound to protect the U.S. Constitution from all enemies, foreign or domestic. Go back to your masters and tell them that I'm coming for them. And in my court, there are no appeals."

Bolan could settle for a stalemate right now, but he knew that there was still a whole war left to fight.

It was a war he'd have to win.

Or they would be the future.

5

The Holiday Inn Express
Roswell, New Mexico

The clock had three hours and twenty-three minutes to burn before the faintest hint of light would be detectable on the horizon. The war council had been in high gear since shortly after its members' arrival around midnight. Aaron Kurtzman had scrambled all available members of Phoenix Force and Able Team to Texas right after notifying Hal Brognola of the emergency signal from Bolan. Rosario "the Politician" Blancanales and Hermann "Gadgets" Schwarz made the flight for Able Team, and only David McCarter stood in for Phoenix Force.

The room was the largest that the hotel had available—two king-size beds, a desk, cable TV, a chest of drawers and a sliding glass door that opened onto a balcony with an excellent view of the highway in both directions. Schwarz had two very large metal suitcases that, when folded open, became a cutting-edge antielectronic surveillance suite. He sat at the desk with his equipment, making sure that the conversation was just between the five of them. He had sensors deployed on the windows, along all wall faces, in every duct and air vent and a small seismic unit sitting on the tile floor in the bathroom. It could detect very easily a drill bit boring a hole through the floor from the room below. Every frequency in the electromagnetic and light spectrums was being monitored for anything unusual.

Schwarz brought everything on line and gave the all-clear. "The only ears that maybe are listening in tonight are God's, ghosts or astral specters."

Blancanales looked at the faces around the room while keeping the Ingram MAC 10 at the ready in his lap. His sector of fire was the balcony. A fat, foot-and-a-half-long suppressor was screwed to the barrel.

"So what's the script, Striker? Is this going to be strictly sideline action?"

"Very strictly sideline."

"I take it, then, that this mission will be, shall we say, very up close and personal?" McCarter speculated.

"Yeah, this work is very personal. When I got back on board with SOG, I reserved the right to pursue missions of my own if I saw the need. I really see the need right now. I can't order any of you to back me up in these plays. This is a volunteer-only operation. This sortie must stay completely outside of SOG support.

"It will be potentially very dicey, because it might appear to the uninformed that we'll be actively attacking individuals in our own government. Our government is in danger of being dissolved by an internal threat. We're a hair's width away from losing the Constitution to the enemy forever. The enemy appears to be the successors to a conspiracy plotted in the last days before Berlin fell to the Allies. Thousands of Nazi scientists, intelligence operatives and high-ranking party members were extended an invitation to join the Allied cold war against communism. Senator John Mannix tells me that this amnesty program was called Operation Paperclip by the OSS. Does that ring anyone's history bells?''

McCarter spoke up. ''Britain's crawling with the Nazi bastards, too. Nobody wants to acknowledge it, either. Seemed like a good idea back then, but in today's politically correct climate, it's a piece of history that nobody wants dredged up. That's probably how the bastards have consolidated their power so quickly and without a ripple in the way of notice. It would be political suicide to even admit that there was a problem.''

''The problem is global now,'' Mannix added. ''They've been quietly dominating the United Nations since they came to America. They're using the generally benevolent perception of the UN by the world's peoples as their duck blind. The bastards are using the treaties clause of the Constitution to ladle more and more of our sovereignty over to the United Nations. They won't be able to come out of the closet with the world reich until American sovereignty has been completely absorbed by the UN Security Council.''

''Man, this shit sounds like the lunatic fringe!'' Schwarz commented. ''Supertabloid special, for Godsake!''

''Unfortunately,'' Bolan said, ''it's not. This is

deadly serious. We were American soldiers, and we all put on our uniforms while taking an oath to defend our freedom, our independence, our way of government from all enemies, foreign or domestic.''

Bolan furrowed his eyebrows, and Blancanales and Schwarz both looked at David McCarter.

In a heartbeat, he caught on to the looks and chuckled. McCarter was British.

''Is that A-okay with you, good buddy?'' Schwarz asked. ''I never heard you take that oath. You guys were on the other side of that issue in the revolution.''

''Yes, we were. Defending the divine right of kings and all that rot. Well, that's got nothing to do with the problem at hand. If Striker needs my help, I'm in.''

Bolan continued. ''Like I said, this war could get very dicey. With what I have seen already and what the senator has briefed me on, my threat assessment is grave. This enemy has to be opposed immediately. These people have the power to trump their hands and force that kind of choice upon me from our own chain of command. Tonight I had wreckage from two of those black helicopters of theirs and the bodies of all their soldiers. We could have learned a lot from that. Even with sanction and my presidential authority to act, when their field operative appeared to claim their property, he got it back. This guy made one phone call, and in less than five minutes, the President himself called me and ordered me to stand down.

''The guy I confronted out there has the same official employer that we do—the federal government. He was the assistant director of the Federal Emergency Management Agency.''

"In a nutshell, we're literally going to war with a federal agency of the U.S. government," Blancanales stated.

Mannix interjected. "Not just any federal agency. Where other federal agencies must at least pay lip service to the Constitution, FEMA's job doesn't even begin until the Constitution is suspended."

"Isn't FEMA that disaster-relief corps I've read about?" McCarter asked.

Mannix took the floor. "FEMA has purposely been associated with disaster relief by the yellow dogs in our media that gleefully cooperate in the dismantling of the Republic. Gentlemen, the Federal Emergency Management Agency exists for one purpose—to provide continuity in government in the event of a national emergency and the declaration of martial law. FEMA agents don't train to hand out toiletries or ease suffering in the wake of a hurricane or an earthquake. They train to seize all government operations, nationalize the economy and organize the population into labor pools to exploit as the nature of the emergency dictates."

"That's one hell of a catch-22, Senator," Blancanales stated. "The federal government, which by law must uphold the Constitution, creates a federal agency that exists to operate government in the absence of the Constitution."

"Yes, it sounds very contradictory. FEMA wouldn't have a legal leg to stand on if it wasn't for the existence of the President's emergency powers. Since World War II, the President's emergency powers have been minutely defined and expanded through successive executive orders from one administration to the next. Under Carter, FEMA was legislated into existence by Congress and handed the job of executing all of the President's emergency powers in the event of a national emergency. Now the concept of a national emergency, you would think, would be clearly and succinctly defined as to what could constitute and what could not constitute the declaration of a national emergency and the suspension of the Constitution. This isn't the case at all. A national emergency is so loosely defined that anything from the wreck of the *Exxon Valdez* to the Speaker of the House having a bad gas day could be trumped up as justification for declaring a national emergency. This is a smoking gun, gentlemen, that we dare not ignore.''

Grimaldi spoke up for the first time. ''Question. If these guys are so big and so bad, why haven't we run afoul of them before now?''

Bolan took back the floor. ''I believe that we have tangled with them on the fringes many times in the past. Back then, we just didn't know what we were looking at. How many times have we locked horns with CIA-backed operations that seem to run contrary to everything the U.S. government is supposed to stand for? The rumors of CIA involvement in the drug trade to finance their black ops off the books, the toppling of democratically elected foreign governments and their replacement with dictatorships. Fascist-style dictatorships that reek of Nazi Germany. It all adds up. When the OSS initiated Operation Paperclip, all of Nazi intelligence was grafted intact into the ranks of the OSS. The CIA replaced the OSS, which means that the CIA inherited the whole bag from the OSS. We didn't beat the Nazis in World War II, we coopted them into our cold war with Soviet communism. And now they're ready to bite the hand that feeds them and declare the Fourth Reich.''

"So what we're looking at are operations now, and maybe in the future, that are completely unofficial, which we conduct on the side while maintaining our usual mission tempo with the Farm. Is that accurate?'' McCarter said.

"Dead accurate,'' Bolan replied. "The fact that our major target is an agency in the federal government makes our identification of the enemy phase of the war even more vital. First we identify the enemy and positively confirm the target as an enemy asset. Only then will we hit it. In the meantime, we'll continue our regular assigned missions. When we have to move on a target, any of you guys who happen to be reaching for something to do when the balloon goes up is welcome to tag along with me and take care of business. That's how I see it playing. We have one mission at hand, but given the far-reaching implications of the conspiracy, I believe this is just the beginning.''

Bolan looked about the faces of the men for comment or constructive criticism.

"Sounds reasonable,'' McCarter said.

"Sign me up, Striker!'' Blancanales told him.

"You can't have a war without reliable communications,'' said Schwarz.

"I'll throw my hat into this ring, as well,'' the

senator added. "I can feed you tips from the crap I see come across my desk every day. I'll be your mole."

"I think this COMCON is going to regret the day that the senator ever gave me a call," Bolan said grimly.

The Rodeway Inn,
Amarillo, Texas

"THIS IS THE MOST disturbing field report you've ever submitted," the chairman lamented.

The chairman looked like a WASP banker and spoke with a New England clip to his words. The leadership of COMCON numbered thirteen, and Joe Newport was one of them. Together they made the executive policy committee of COMCON. These thirteen men stayed scattered about the globe most of the time, coming together only on occasions like this one, when major operations were ready to go active and decisions had to be made, marching orders cut.

The meeting being called in the Panhandle was no happenstance decision. A major operation, Chaos Theory, was ready to go green, and the committee had to grant final authorization.

When the need arose for the COMCON elite to gather, an out-of-the-way conference room was secured in a second-rate hotel near the area of operations by a bogus "multilevel marketing company" for their regional sales convention. It was a flawless cover, really. MLMs were running rampant all over the country in an economy rife with instability and corporate layoffs.

Newport sat alone on one side of the table, while everyone else sat across from him, staring with little expression. He shook a cigarette free and stuck it in his mouth.

"I'm as concerned by this as you are," Newport replied.

The chairman sat at the center of the table. The third man to his left, code-named Methuselah and just as old, interjected. "How might this affect the Texas trigger point you previously reported was ready to activate?"

"I anticipate no changes."

"Yet your current assessment reveals that an unknown party or parties may now have our scent and might be presently planning to interfere with our goals."

"I blindsided them completely yesterday. If it wasn't for those two hotshots that decided to take their own initiative and keep me out of the loop until it was too late, I might have been able to maintain total containment."

"Your opponent seems to be apt at recovering from blindsidedness," the chairman said.

"My opponent doesn't know shit, Mr. Chairman. He knows nothing of our methods and has nothing to strike at. He's seen a couple of helicopters and some private troops. That's about all this smart guy has to go on right now, because I took the evidence away from him."

"Yes, and that's another troubling part of your

report. Why didn't this operative just kill you and take it anyway?''

"I don't know if this guy is on contract or if he's with a real executive-action unit that we weren't aware of until now. The fact is that this Pollock was operating on orders from the President himself, and he couldn't very well gun down another federal agent without extreme provocation, and I offered none. If this guy is working for the Feds, that's something I can exploit. I'm going to track him back to his commanding agency and shut his smart ass down at the source.''

"The fact that this unknown agency could escape our notice is unsettling,'' Methuselah clucked.

The chairman said, "You have full authorization to neutralize this threat to the reich. However, do not bring attention on us in any way. Keep it very discreet and very deniable.''

"The motto of my section, I assure you.''

"What of the civilian photographer that escaped with photographs of the AeroDeth?'' the man code-named Spartacus asked.

Newport looked at his watch. "As of this moment, I imagine that the Gumps are in a world of hurt.''

Odessa, Texas

HOMER GUMP WAS in his unfinished basement, applying the final touches to an e-mail to Richard T. Kirkland of *Soldier of Fortune* magazine. He didn't mention money. He knew that the man would want to see the goods first, probably want to analyze the images, too, before any talk of money would be discussed. He was attaching one decent cropped digital image of the black helicopter to act as the bait when there was a crash above him, Lillian's startled scream and a sound that chilled his blood—rancorous laughter.

Gump's outstretched finger was poised two inches above the enter key when bedlam erupted upstairs, and rather than take the extra half second to strike the key and fire the message across cyberspace, Gump reacted like any good family man would.

He lurched out of his chair and raced across the open basement to the walnut rifle cabinet that was always padlocked in the name of child safety. He flicked the lock up dumbly, wondering what the hell he was doing, then stabbed his hand into his pocket for the keys.

At the top of the stairs, the door banged open and a sneering teenage voice taunted loudly, "Hey, Pops! We're here for the pictures!" Heavy boot heels clubbed the bare wood on a stampeding descent.

Gump flipped through the keys on the ring frantically. He found the right key and was trying to get it in the lock when the steel-toed boot tip connected with his right kidney. Gump's head exploded with pain. He screamed, lost his grip on everything and fell to the hard concrete in a yawn of blackness.

Strong hands grabbed his T-shirt and roughly flipped him on his back.

Gump groaned and blinked his eyes rapidly to clear his vision.

The leering face of his attacker swam into focus;

the punk couldn't have been more than eighteen years old. The stubble on his otherwise bald head hinted that he was a blonde, and the scabs of multiple nicks on his cranium attested to his expertise with a disposable shaver. The Iron Cross flittered under his left lobe on an honest-to-God fishhook.

The punk's eyes were wild and gray.

He wore a battered black leather jacket that looked as if it had been used as a makeshift mud flap in another life. A ragged T-shirt advertising an obscure racist metal band was either too big or this punk wasn't much in the muscles department. He had a motorcycle chain for a belt, greasy jeans and engineer boots that biker gangs loved to wear as auxiliary weapons systems.

The reeking bastard leaned in close so his image would overwhelm Gump's visual cortex.

"Where're the pictures, you old fuck?"

The punk hit Gump in the face with tattooed knuckles.

"You better start talkin'!"

Gump's lips moved, but nothing came out. His eyes were bugging and bobbing on a sea of tears, and he fought hard to use his eyes and look away from the skinhead monster and focus his eyes on the Internet workstation across the basement, behind them. The punk picked up the cue quick; he looked over his shoulder and saw the computer hardware.

"They over there?"

Gump nodded as best he could. The gesture amounted to nothing more than a slight lift of the old skull, coming up an inch maybe, to fall back with a thud, completely spent. The waves of pain crashed against his brain, and he couldn't find anywhere to hide from it. His kidney was hamburger. He knew that. Death was unavoidable. He knew that, too. He'd linger with this one, the final blackness seeping in slowly like a Chinese water torture. He knew that about himself. He was a sticker.

The punk stalked up on the computer workstation like a primitive encountering something completely unfamiliar. The e-mail software was the active window, and the cropped .JPG of the helicopter occupied a large box on the screen, anchored to the message and queued ready to send.

"What's this runnin' here? How do I turn this off?"

The punk's computer illiteracy rate had to have been off the scale. He had no clue that the Esc key meant "escape." He did what a lot of people would have done when confronted with the computer keyboard for the first time: he began the random hunt-and-peck strategy, hoping to strike a key that would close the program. He found that active key when he hit Enter.

"Hey, it's doin' somethin' here."

A message box popped open in the middle of the screen: "Mail being sent. Mail sent."

"Shit! What the fuck did this thing do?"

Gump would have laughed out loud if it wasn't for the nerve-scrambling pain that dominated every cell in his body. Maybe it was the knowledge that he was a dead man that granted the lucidity to see a way to further the damage done, to make sure that the truth had a fighting chance of leaking out.

He struggled to sit up and was only successful in rolling onto his side and onto an elbow.

"Help me...help...me up," Gump croaked.

The punk continued frantically striking the keyboard, trying to undo what couldn't be undone.

"What the fuck did I do? Make this piece of shit stop!"

"Help me up...just help me."

The skinhead stomped back to Gump, glaring down at the man. He knelt and grabbed Gump by the collar, yanking him up onto unsteady feet.

"You make this fuckin' thing do what I want!"

"Just help me...over there."

The punk dragged Gump to the workstation.

Clutching the edge of the desk with both hands to steady himself, Gump then reached out with his left hand and began to paw through the scattered floppies littering the open space on the desk. He picked up the one labeled in big, precise letters, Pictures, West Texas.

He held it up, over his shoulder, to the hovering skinhead.

"This is the disk. The pictures, everything...is on it."

The punk snatched the disk out of Gump's weak fingers and pocketed it inside his leather jacket.

"What did I just do on that fuckin' thing?"

"You sent an e-mail," Gump grunted.

"With that picture on it?"

"Ah, yes. The picture was attached."

"Where'd it go?"

"It went to Richard T. Kirkland."

"Who the fuck is he?"

"Publisher of *Soldier of Fortune* magazine."

"Fuck! Fuck! Fuck!"

"Unless...unless you have a patsy working that magazine, I guess you're pretty well screwed now, mister."

"Shut up! Can you get it back?"

Gump shook his head, then dropped to his knees in pain.

"This the only disk?"

Gump nodded.

"You're lyin'!"

Gump shook his head again.

"I have nothing to lie about, mister," Gump panted. "I'm a dead man anyway."

"You're right about that, Pops."

"Just leave my family alone. Please. You got what you came for."

"We ain't got near what we came for, Pops. Now let's go see that family of yours."

6

Tranquillity Base,
Northern Louisiana

The night-vision goggles made spotting the video cameras and the crisscrossing laser-beam barriers a lot easier in the dark. Mack Bolan was in combat blacksuit and armed for a soft probe that might go hard. In case that happened, the M-16/M-203 combo was primed and ready, slung across his back. He picked his way through the vine-choked pines, avoiding the obstacles by boxing around them until he came to the edge of the immaculate lawn that engulfed the administrative building in a homogeneous green island surrounded by towering, botanical chaos.

The administrative wing of Tranquillity Base was housed in the plantation mansion that had been on the property since before the Civil War. The place had been a cotton farm back then and had remained a cotton farm until a fire-and-brimstone preacher came along who called himself the Apostle of God, aka Jock Macon, and bought the place in 1982. The Apostle—who had his own radio show—turned the place into a private juvenile ''correctional facility'' almost immediately and constantly referred over the airwaves to his "court of the last resort" for frantic Christian parents of teens in the clutches of Satan. Christian parents in a money crunch were extended a financing option at a generous twenty-one percent interest rate for the cost of a one-year stay for their Satan-seduced teen. Multiple-teen internee rates were also available upon request.

Above all, the Apostle boasted of results. He sent home shining little models of Christian obedience and respect.

He had miles of testimonial video footage in the archives of his "graduates" back in their homes leading super Christian lives happily subservient to their parents.

The huge plantation house was maintained to historical-society standards. Teen-internee work crews kept the mansion and the greens tip-top. Constant trimming, mowing, weed pulling and repainting took place every day except Sunday. Sunday was the Lord's Day. The teens spent long, grueling days rotating between indoctrination classes and work crews doing hard labor in the fields and around the compound.

Tranquillity Base was an economic juggernaut on the balance sheet and lined the mysterious board of directors' pockets with cold cash deposited into offshore accounts. The money paid to the church for the right to work their teen trustees like slaves six days a week for a year was chump change compared to the money earned from the sales of the cotton and tobacco grown in church fields and tended by free labor, the designer jeans and lingerie assembled in the sweatshop and sold by mail and party plan. In another wing of the sweatshop, teens spent hours bottling and boxing the herbal-vitamin products that the Apostle hawked to an eager army of network marketing devotees thru a MLM company owned and endorsed by the church. The Apostle had a couple of long haired scientists on retainer to formulate the company's potions and vitamin supplements.

Tranquillity Base was a money machine and a mini-slave state all rolled up into one monstrous aberration of the capitalist system. The church's black payroll ate up twenty-three percent of the church's operating costs and provided lots of extra folding green to line the wallets of local politicos and cops.

The church had carte blanche immunity to prey.

The Apostle's hard-core faithful in the church weren't any wiser about the dark side of Tranquillity Base and maintained a steady flow of revenue under the constant barrage from the pulpit that was a mix of Armageddon theology and political paranoia.

The Executioner was on to them.

Bolan studied the plantation house through the NVGs and identified two rotating cameras immediately. The cameras were equipped with little infrared lights that turned the night into day. He could see the IR lights with the NVGs. One camera was mounted on the side of the house that covered his approach. The second was mounted on the razor-wire-topped fence, looking into the property. Both cameras would see him the minute he emerged from the wood line.

He'd have to neutralize the cameras before he could make his approach on the administrative building. Most of the windows in the place were brightly lit; the administrative section kept odd hours.

Bolan needed to identify the man in charge, and that would require close-up snooping, looking and listening.

Once he solved the camera problem first.

He drew the 93-R from a nose-down fast-draw shoulder holster that had been designed to accommodate the weapon with the suppressor screwed to the barrel and the laser sighting device Bolan had added just for this mission. He activated the beam and aimed at the camera mounted to the mansion. Through his goggles, he could see the camera housing panning back and forth with green-hued digital clarity. He located the bright dot his laser beam was making on the side of the house and moved the dot to cover the space where the camera lens would be when the camera panned back toward him.

He let out his breath and paused, pulling some slack out of the trigger.

He fired off a 3-round burst when the laser dot was to the right edge of the camera. The rounds shattered the lens and blew apart the face. Bolan assessed the damage through the NVGs. The camera continued to rotate, but its image-processing unit was hanging out.

He swung around and targeted the second camera. Three more subsonic coughs and another video monitor somewhere switched to snow.

Bolan sprinted across the open lawn and avoided the spill illumination from the bright halogen lights that lit up the front gate and guard shack. He went low at the flower beds and flattened against the house. With the light coming from the windows and the white paint on the oak siding, Bolan presented an easily seen silhouette. Fortunately a line of shoulder-high shrubs ran almost the entire side of the house. If he stayed between the house and the shrubs, he would remain largely unseen. He rose just enough to peer into the window above him. The louvers were drawn, but he could see through the cracks that the office inside was empty. He dipped back down and went to the next window. Another empty office.

The Executioner hit paydirt in the last office from the end. The louvers were open and two men were in the spacious office, staying close to the wet bar. One of the men was the Apostle himself. The other man was a complete unknown.

Bolan affixed a small microphone to the corner of the window with an adhesive and turned on the listening device. The device sent its input to the earpiece of Bolan's radio and to a small microcassette recorder snugged into a pouch on his assault vest. The soldier adjusted the volume and listened in on what the two men were discussing.

After a few minutes, Bolan knew he had a viable target here.

JOCK MACON POURED more Scotch whiskey into his glass and turned to face Morty Zimmerman, the COMCON lawyer who was handling the Kyler Applegate fiasco for the church. Kyler Applegate was a sixteen-year-old native of Midland, Texas, who lived with her grandmother, her legal guardian.

Some kind of territorial spat took place between the grandmother and granddaughter, and Kyler took a bus to Alexandria, Louisiana, to live with her father, an unemployed janitor. It didn't take long for the two to mutually hate each other and one night while on a drunken binge, Daddy came home, beat Kyler and sexually assaulted her.

When he sobered up, he panicked. He couldn't think of any other way to keep her quiet than killing her. He kept her tied to a chair for two days while he wrestled with how he was going to kill her so no suspicion would fall on him. On the morning of the third day, he saw the Apostle's late-night cablecast and heard about the wonderful, private, Christian-administered incarceration camp for teens gone bad called Tranquillity Base.

He immediately phoned the 1-888 line and told the "counselor" about his wild, uncontrollable, drug-sniffing daughter who he suspected was starring in porno flicks. He told the counselor that he was at his wits end, and that he didn't want his daughter back after a year—he wanted to sign her over in perpetuity. Forever.

The Apostle accepted those terms at no cost. The project was always looking for kids they could get full custody of. They became wards of the Apostle's private state and guinea pigs for Project Monarch.

Daddy drugged Kyler with five tablets of over-the-counter Tranquil and drove her to Tranquillity Base in the dead of night. He signed the pages of documents drafted by church attorney Morty Zimmerman, and left his daughter and his worries in the Apostle's firm hands.

FREE FREE
BOOKS! GIFT!

PLAY BANGO!

AND CLAIM 2 FREE BOOKS
AND A FREE GIFT!

BANGO
5 19 32 54 73
6 17 41 50 6
13 22 FREE 52
5 24 44 46
8 21 35 47 75

BANGO
9 19 44 52 71
4 20 32 50 68
11 18 FREE 53 63
7 27 36 60 72
3 28 41 47 64

★ No Cost!
★ No Obligation to Buy!
★ No Purchase Necessary!

TURN THE PAGE TO PLAY

PLAY BANGO!
AND GET THREE FREE GIFTS!

It looks like BINGO, it plays like BINGO but it's FREE

HOW TO PLAY:

1. With a coin, scratch the Caller Card to reveal your 5 lucky numbers and see that they match your Bango Card. Then check the claim chart to discover what we have for you — 2 FREE BOOKS and a FREE GIFT — ALL YOURS, ALL FREE!

2. Send back the Bango card and you'll get two hot-off-the press Gold Eagle® novels. These books have a cover price of $4.50 or more each, but they are yours to keep absolutely free.

3. There's no catch. You're under no obligation to buy anything. We charge nothing — ZERO — for your first shipment. And you don't have to make any minimum number of purchases — not even one!

4. The fact is, thousands of readers enjoy receiving our books by mail from the Gold Eagle Reader Service™ months before they are available in stores. They like the convenience of home delivery and they love our discount prices!

5. We hope that after receiving your free books you'll want to remain a subscriber. But the choice is yours — to continue or cancel, any time at all! So why not take us up on our invitation, with no risk of any kind. You'll be glad you did!

YOURS FREE!
This exciting mystery gift is yours free when you play BANGO!

It's fun, and we're giving away
FREE GIFTS
to all players!

PLAY BANGO!

CALLER CARD

SCRATCH → HERE!

YES! Please send me the 2 free books and the gift for which I qualify! I understand that I am under no obligation to purchase any books as explained on the back of this card.

YOUR CARD ↓

BANGO

B	A	N	G	O
38	9	44	10	38
92	7	5	27	14
2	51	FREE	91	67
75	3	12	20	13
6	15	26	50	31

CLAIM CHART!

Match 5 numbers	2 FREE BOOKS & A MYSTERY GIFT
Match 4 numbers	2 FREE BOOKS
Match 3 numbers	1 FREE BOOK

(MB-OS-09/00)

366 ADL C4H3   **166 ADL C4H2**

NAME   (PLEASE PRINT CLEARLY)

ADDRESS

APT.#   CITY

STATE/PROV.   ZIP/POSTAL CODE

The Gold Eagle Reader Service™ — Here's how it works:

If offer card is missing write to: Gold Eagle Reader Service, 3010 Walden Ave., P.O. Box 1867, Buffalo, NY 14240-1867

BUSINESS REPLY MAIL

FIRST-CLASS MAIL   PERMIT NO. 717   BUFFALO, NY

POSTAGE WILL BE PAID BY ADDRESSEE

GOLD EAGLE READER SERVICE
3010 WALDEN AVE
PO BOX 1867
BUFFALO NY 14240-9952

NO POSTAGE
NECESSARY
IF MAILED
IN THE
UNITED STATES

A week later, his ex-mother-in-law, Kyler's grandmother, began ringing the phone off the hook night and day. He could only tell the pushy bitch that Kyler wasn't there so many times. On day four, he cracked and told her that Kyler was a sniveling, Satan-possessed harlot of Babylon and that he'd sent her away to a place that was going to help her kick the Satan habit. Grandmother Cornelia van Horn wasn't a religious lunatic, and she knew her former son-in-law wasn't religious. The lunatic part still applied. So the fundamentalist psychobabble came off sounding very wrong.

Another couple days of chipping away squeezed out the name of the camp Kyler was in.

Cornelia had all she needed to launch a one-grandmother crusade to free Kyler from Tranquillity Base. Her first pilgrimage to the private prison earned her ten days in county lockup, the knowledge that Ronnie Applegate had illegally signed over his daughter to Jock Macon completely, and when released, was escorted to the county line by sheriff's deputies like an enemy of the state.

When she got back to Midland, she wasted no time in contacting reporters and telling her story. The story ran in the Sunday-through-Wednesday editions. It was picked up off the wire by ten states in the southwestern region and quickly became a seminational controversy. Nosy reporters began to show up at the front gate, wanting interviews, wanting to see the kids, wanting to see Kyler.

Jock Macon tried to appease them with stalling sound bites about the matter being under review by church attorneys. Cornelia returned in the midst of the flurry and pitched a pup tent in the grass on the other side of the road from the front gate and spent a week marching up and down the country lane picketing for her granddaughter's release.

In Cornelia van Horn, the Apostle had a tiger by the tail.

The media went crazy over the picketing stunt, and the Apostle had to shut down a lot of the more blatant sweatshop activities until the uproar abated. The focus of the public eye began to cut badly into profits.

Then one day Morty Zimmerman walked up to the Apostle and told him, "The Committee has authorized the release of Kyler Applegate."

The Apostle wasn't used to their taking things away, or to their knuckling under to media scrutiny.

Seeing one of their key operational facilities on the nightly news had to be taking a toll at the top. Above all else, the COMCON leadership maintained strict discretion in every operation drawn up and activated. No one was to draw any attention whatsoever to the organization.

"What about her mission? She won't be ready if we let her go back now."

"The Committee instructed Aquarius to step up her training. His last report states that she is ready."

"It'd be nice to be let in on your basic important info once in a while, Morty."

"You're told only what you need to know. You're an employee, Mr. Macon. You're not a planner or a field operative. Instead of the public seeing us, they see you. That is the purpose you serve."

Once the employee was reminded of his relative

position in the pecking order, the leadership's messenger went on to give Macon his marching orders. On May 5, around 3:00 a.m., Cornelia van Horn was being flown directly to Tranquillity Base's landing strip, where she would be speedily linked up with Kyler. They'd reboard the aircraft and fly back to Midland. After that, Kyler was in the apt hands of field operatives for Chaos Theory, and that was all that Macon needed to know.

Macon twirled his whiskey around in his glass and glanced at his watch—3:10.

"Why in the hell are we doing this so damned early?"

"No reporters are up at three o'clock in the morning. It's dark. There's less for that old bitch to snoop into."

"And Aquarius won't keep me updated on anything he's doing down there. The son of a bitch never comes out of that hole. How do you know he hasn't gone insane down there? You need somebody to audit things around here, make sure everything runs on schedule."

"And you would be the logical choice for such a position."

"I know this place administratively. Administration is administration."

"Yes, indeed. First, Colonel Aquarius isn't required to keep you abreast of anything, Mr. Macon. The colonel reports to the Committee. As to expanding your sphere of responsibility and letting you see more than you've already seen by becoming our auditor of operations—we value you where you are, Mr. Macon. This is where you serve us best."

"I guess it's going to take that psycho down there to completely flake out and send a bunch of your hypnotized androids off half cocked before you'll say 'we should have had an auditor.'"

"You're confusing your functions with mine, Mr. Macon."

"Is that what you do around here?"

"Your curiosity is disturbing. It's not a good idea to disturb us like that."

"Okay, I get the picture."

"Your willingness to want to do more for our cause is commendable. There's a place for men like you in the world to come."

"Yeah, just don't forget that."

These men he'd chosen to associate with were notorious for suddenly ending relationships—permanently. They promised the Jewel of the Nile and delivered with a bullet to the brainpan. Or worse. The lucky ones were canceled through the barrel of a gun. The damned souls went down into the hole, into Aquarius's realm.

While contemplating his martini, Zimmerman said, "Please hand me the phone."

He wanted to refuse, but thought better of it and handed it over.

Zimmerman took the console, looked distastefully at the clumsy toy with all the bells and whistles and handed the executive telephone center back to Macon while keeping the receiver in his hand.

"Dial the hole for me."

Macon dialed the extension, marveling at his own willingness to roll over and be somebody's bitch.

Zimmerman waited two rings for someone to answer.

"It's me. Zimmerman. Is the girl ready to travel?"

Macon couldn't hear Aquarius respond.

The lawyer nodded to whatever the answer was. "Is she ready to be activated immediately?"

Aquarius was most likely pontificating upon his immenseness within the occult realm of psycho-science and mind rape.

"You're positive, then."

More indignation and outrage at the thought.

"Then I'll let our people in Midland know the good news. Very good. I never had any doubts, but I have to ask the questions."

Zimmerman handed the receiver back to Macon, who hung up and put the phone center back on his desk.

"Everything is on schedule, Mr. Macon. All without the services of an auditor, too."

SOMEBODY ALWAYS had to be at the security station no matter what was going on anywhere else. Every morning between 3:00 a.m. and 5:00 a.m., security protocol took a little coffee break and the graveyard guard detail gathered in the holding-cell block and engaged in the kind of fun and games that were punishable by law.

Colonel Gabriel Aquarius had taken a special liking to his graveyard boys, who guarded the gateway to Hell topside after the witching hour. His graveyard boys treated him with the utmost respect, which befitted a man with his great abilities.

As a gesture of his gratitude, he allowed his boys to sexually assault his most recent mind-control candidate for two hours in the early hours of most mornings.

However, Lonnie Morgan wasn't part of the rotation this a.m. He was pulling watch at the security station. Nine minutes remained on his shift, then he'd be tagged out to go and join the sexual assault that he was watching on monitor 4.

Morgan didn't notice monitors 12 and 13 were full of electronic snow. His gaze was locked on to monitor 4. He wished the camera were maneuverable so he could get just the right angle on the action.

He glanced at the clock on the wall outside the security station to see how much time was left before he could join the action. That's when he noticed the two monitors were no longer monitoring anything. He swiveled his chair so he could face that bank of monitors and began to fiddle with the adjustment knobs. Nothing responded. It was probably a loose cable or something, but protocol demanded that somebody take a physical look at those two cameras.

And it wasn't going to be Lonnie Morgan.

He turned to face the communications console, then activated the intercom into the holding-cell block.

He spoke into the microphone. "Franken-Boner, you have two seconds to pull out, get your trousers secure and report to this station. Franken-Boner, report!"

On monitor number 4, Franken-Boner exited the

cell. In the security station, a bell went off and Franken-Boner growled, "What the hell is this, Lonnie? What's going on?"

"Franken-Boner, bud, you're going to have to go outside now and visually check cameras 12 and 13."

"Let the next guy in the rotation check it out."

"The next guy in the rotation, Franken-Boner, will be manning my post, I'll be having my turn with that hot number, and you'll be giving my relief a report via radio about what you see out there at cameras 12 and 13. Is that all very clear to you, Franken-Boner?"

"Yeah, shit!"

A moment later, Franken-Boner shuffled out of the cellblock. He glared through the thick glass of the security station at Lonnie Morgan, who waved with a smile. Franken-Boner flipped him the bird, then strapped on his utility belt and clipped his radio's mike to his left shoulder epaulet. He gripped the butt of his revolver and wiggled it to make sure the weapon was strapped down tight. He pulled the key card out of his shirt and stuck the card into a reader slot next to the exit hatch. The little red light became a little green light, the pressure seals burst on the hatch and the door popped out on hinges and slid to the side.

Franken-Boner stepped through the hatch and into the cool humidity.

THROUGH THE EARPIECE the ringing phone sounded much louder to Bolan than it probably was in the actual room. Morty Zimmerman answered the phone on the first ring, hoping it was word from the airfield that the plane was on approach.

It was the security station at the bunker reporting the downed cameras.

Zimmerman hung up and turned to Jock Macon, standing in the corner by a fern sipping his whiskey in contemplation.

"A couple of cameras have suddenly gone down. They're sending some guys to check it out."

Macon grunted. He wasn't interested.

Bolan bristled. They'd finally noticed the cameras.

He broke down his listening post and eased himself into the thickest clump of shrubbery he could find. He holstered the Beretta and pulled a combat knife off his vest. Being so close to the window and the men inside, he had to exercise extra stealth in the kill. Firing the Beretta, even with the suppressor, might make enough noise to blow the soft probe.

The Executioner wasn't ready to go hard just yet.

His earpiece crackled to life.

"Striker, this is Cover Story. I have a sentry moving out into the open about one hundred yards south of you and heading in your direction."

It was David McCarter. He was in ghillie suit and hunkered down in the tall grass on the other side of the road, looking into the compound through the front gate. He'd set up his sniper position almost directly to the rear of where Cornelia van Horn had pitched her pup tent on her second pilgrimage to Tranquillity Base a couple months before.

"I've got him," Bolan whispered.

"Do you want him taken out?"

"Negative. Let him come to me."

"Roger."

Bolan listened to the guy close the gap, talking into his radio. He was almost to the flower beds when Bolan heard him report, "Lonnie, the camera is still rotating and... What is that? Looks like something is hanging off the box. Let me get under it. Hold on."

The beefy security guard waded into the bushes. He looked up at the camera mount and clicked his mike button at the same time.

"Hey, Lonnie! I think—"

Bolan hit him from behind. He hooked his left forearm under the man's chin and yanked the guy's head back, locking his jaws shut while driving the six-inch combat blade into the man's kidney with his right fist and twisting the blade violently. The guard stiffened and gagged before relaxing with a shudder. Bolan pulled the knife out and lowered the body to the dirt.

The radio mike clipped to the man's epaulet crackled with static.

"Franken-Boner! Say again, over! I don't copy! Franken-Boner!"

Bolan unclipped the mike and raised it to his lips.

"Lonnie, yeah. Sorry for the scare. It's nothing. Looks like some vines or something that got blown on the camera."

"You sure? Can you get them off?"

"Hold on."

Bolan waited five seconds, then said, "There. How's that?"

"Nothing. It's still just a screen full of snow."

"Maybe it's on your end."

"I don't know."

"I'm going to walk the perimeter while I'm out here."

"You're what?"

"I'm going to check the perimeter. Just so we're covered."

"You're a good man, Franken-Boner, going the extra mile. Give us a report in five, ten minutes."

"Sure. Out."

Bolan tossed the mike onto the corpse's chest and dragged the body deeper into the brush. He had some breathing room now.

He keyed his throat mike.

"All stations, change of roster. We're pulling out. Regroup with Mother Goose and await further instructions. How copy, over?"

"Good copy, out," McCarter replied.

Schwarz and Blancanales sent the same message.

The Executioner retraced his steps to the wood line. He stepped through the shadow-wall of the trees and became invisible again, wrapped in darkness.

KYLER APPLEGATE'S designation while in the hole was 777.

Aquarius had been the totality of her universe for ninety-three days running. Not all the kids incarcerated at Tranquillity Base ever did time in the hole. In-processing paperwork of each new "candidate" included extensive psychological testing and questioning. If an adolescent was discovered to have a history of abuse, sexual or physical, that kid's jacket went down the hole and Aquarius examined the data critically.

By the time the new inmate cleared administration, the kid was already assigned to the hole, if judged a worthy retrainee. If not, the inmate stayed aboveground, was assigned a bunk in one of the open-bay dormitories and joined the general population. There was no whispered warning among the general population to new arrivals to steer clear of the hole. The abovegrounders didn't even know that there was a much darker side to Tranquillity Base than the one they were seeing.

They were being scientifically segregated the minute their shadows darkened the administration doorway.

Life inside the hole was a surreal nightmare that had a very lethal method to all the madness. The place was a factory for scientifically shredding psyches and gaining total mind control over the retrainees. Mass mind control from birth was a hallmark of the new civilization, the civilization that the reich would administer. The pundits and sympathizers of this vision gushed enthusiastically over the new possibility, one that humankind never had before now: the prospect of "psycho-civilizing" the whole lot.

A world with no violence, no war, no "undesirables." Individuality, sense of self beyond the self deemed fit for the state, would be the casualties in a perfect world.

This would be the price for world peace.

The decision to proceed with Operation Paperclip and integrate intact Germany's intelligence and scientific organizations, putting them to work in the cause of America, was an unexpected boon for the burgeoning national-security state. The fledgling Nazi mind-control technology was picked up and subsidized by the American intelligence community.

The cryptocracy was very interested in developing a remote mind-control technology that could be rolled out on a global scale and introduced via channels that were already in place and trusted blindly by the masses. They wanted a microchip that could regulate chemical exchanges in the brain and turn off the electrochemical transactions that underlay all human behaviors, such as aggression, territoriality, rebellion and hatred. The microchip would also augment and encourage the electrochemical exchanges that resulted in docility, contentment and the inability to disobey the orders of anybody identified as a master. The chip would have to be incredibly small so that the favored method of introduction into the general population could be utilized at no cost: U.S.- and UN-funded vaccination programs that were in the process of being legally declared mandatory for all.

Prototypes of just such a chip were already being field-tested by the WHO in several central African nations that were textbook examples of instability, civil war and rampaging overpopulation.

The latest design twist in the chip was still in laboratory testing stages. This current generation of the technology promised to give the cryptocracy molecular-level control over the unapproved passions of the masses. Nanotechnology would give them what they were looking for. The microchip was now deployed into the subject's bloodstream with an army of nanites—molecular-size "machines" capable of interfering with the individual neurons to suppress the behaviors the cryptocracy deemed unhealthy for society, while supporting those behaviors the shadow rulers saw as being manageable. The microchip now acted as a central command center, directing its nanite minions by radio transmission. The RF signal was very tiny; the designers needed a range of about a foot in any direction so that the mother chip could remain in constant contact with her billions of independent hands and fingers.

The implications and applications of the dawning era of nanotechnology went far beyond mind control of the unruly masses—humankind was now on the threshold of physical immortality and mortal godhood while wielding these powers with the disposition of an enraged toddler. Technological knowhow had far outstripped wisdom, and many people would suffer because of this deficit in the cosmic ledger.

This new generation of technology made the ancient, arcane techniques perfected over millennia for making zombie slaves out of individuals unnecessary. The advances were lauded, funded and encouraged to further refinement while the old ways, handed down adept to neophyte for generations to the initiates of the Black Lodge, were still part of their ritual drama and religion.

The inner circle of COMCON, the mysterious men who were at the very capstone in the organizational pyramid, were all initiates of the same Black Order that the ringleaders of the Nazi Party were fanatical devotees of. It was called the Thule

Society in Nazi Germany. Thule's modern-day protégés called it the Order of the Midnight Sun, but the secret religion remained unchanged. Captured documents from the war gave the false impression that Thule's occultism was based in the Nordic pantheon of the Germanic people's pagan past. The religion of the Midnight Sun was older than that; it antedated any other human religion on the planet. The initiates of Thule guarded their religion and its gods jealously from the profane. They coded their religion behind the names and myths of their Nordic ancestors in much the same way that practitioners of Santeria used the Catholic saints to hide their voodoo gods.

There was a global cult of very powerful people who worshiped the infernal Old Ones, and their faith was expressed politically through fascism. And since World War II, another version of the domino theory had been marching forth steadily and largely unreported. The list of U.S.-equipped, trained and supported fascist client states in the Third World, particularly in Central and South America, seemed more the result of design than anything resembling the proverbial coincidence.

The time was near.

Colonel Gabriel Aquarius was a man of the times. Society was in flux, the rules were changing and everywhere uncertainty and fear of the future were pandemic. Which was quite in line with what he knew of the extracosmic forces that were fueling the collapse of the old order.

He was a career officer in the United States Army Reserve and had branched into psychological operations upon completing Officer Candidate School at Fort Benning, Georgia. He'd been a visionary in psy-ops, elevating it out of the era of leaflet scattering and loudspeaker appeals to peasant masses and into the realm of super-sci-fi mind war.

His lifelong interest in the dark side of reality drew him like a moth to the flame of the arcane and the occult. He'd once been a member of Anton LaVey's Church of Satan, which ended in exile when he came to perceive that LaVey's gang was more interested in circus-sideshow hedonism than in really forging the iron links that would usher in the Age of Satan. His own researches and experimentations were calling into question the legitimacy of exalting a religion around the archnemesis of the Judeo-Christian God. To accept the objective reality of Satan was to acknowledge the de facto existence of the Judeo-Christian deity. One couldn't exist in the vacuum of the other.

So he broke away, founded the Temple of Seitan and buried the matter by adopting a deity of darkness that antedated the theological treadmill of God and Satan. The cult was international in scope and made no bones about its spiritual adoption of the occult interests of the Third Reich as a matter of importance to its working charter, but publicly distanced itself from the political and sociological aspects of Nazism. Yet the Nazi movement itself was a direct machination of those very occult beliefs of Himmler and his ilk. The posturing on this issue was nothing more than balm to soothe the easily convinced.

Aquarius stood at the security station console

where he'd taken the call from the surface. Those prattling fools on the Committee would be years behind in their timetables if it wasn't for the singular light of his genius to provide the wares of their ambitions. He'd once again provided them with their sacrificial goat on a lunatic schedule. Rather than heap the praises of his immense abilities to crank out perfect agents of terrorism and chaos, Zimmerman wanted to know if Kyler Applegate was ready yet. As if there were some doubt as to whether he could deliver as promised.

He raised his hand and made a come-here gesture over his shoulder to the security guard behind him. The drone snapped into action and quick-timed around Aquarius to face the tall, intimidating figure in black.

"Yes, my lord."

"Prepare 777. Her time has come."

The sentry hurried away, then halted in front of a large steel door and inserted a security card into the reader on the wall to the right. The red light on the panel winked out, and a green light next to it lit up. There was a soft whirring as motors and servos came to life, and the doors parted with a hiss. The sentry into the corridor beyond, eerily lit by soft blue light panels in the ceiling.

THE EXECUTIONER MADE his way through the main compound, staying just inside the tree line, and remained alert for laser trip beams and security cameras. The night air still had the chill of winter, and the atmospheric conditions of the dark morning were excellent for conducting sound over a distance. The forests of northern Louisiana were choked with constricting vegetation and wait-a-minute vines. Bolan used his fingertips, as well as his NVGs, to locate the botanical obstacles in his path and negotiate the quickest and quietest way through. Stealth was paramount now, as he couldn't afford to alert the enemy to his presence before he could call for an extraction.

He made it into the back forty without incident. He stepped just outside of the tree line and dropped to one knee to survey the layout of the private airfield. Against the black wall of the forest, the Executioner was nearly invisible. The airfield had been constructed in the middle of a large open meadow, and the forest at both ends of the runway had been pushed back to add more length to the concrete strip. The outline of the runway was suddenly described with green, blue and red points of light, and the Executioner ticked off a rough estimate of the landing strip's length.

A C-130 could be landed there with tarmac to spare. If Tranquillity Base were really just a private behavior-correction facility run by a fire-and-brimstone preacher, Bolan could see no need for the airfield spread out before him. Supplies were easily trucked in by road. What possible reason could there be for justifying an airfield that could land military transports covertly at this private facility?

Bolan couldn't think of anything legitimate. But on the illegitimate side of the question, he could easily think of a dozen things that might be going on behind this smoke screen of Christian tough love. He didn't like any of those possibilities.

A vehicle engine roared to life on his backtrail,

sounding like the Jeep Cherokee he saw parked in the lot of the administration building. It'd be Macon and the lawyer. A single-lane dirt road bisected the compound, running from the front gate to the airfield, and ended at the concrete taxi apron on Bolan's side of the meadow. A large maintenance hangar was coming to life. Light posts horseshoeing the structure flickered on, and the doors slid aside. A baggage tractor rolled onto the apron, pulling two carts behind it. Several men in white coveralls milled in front of the hangar, and a guy with earphones and cone flashlights strode forward to guide the plane in once it had landed.

In the distance to the east, Bolan heard the faint growl of turbine jet engines, gaining in volume as the plane closed on final approach.

He spoke into his throat mike.

"Mother Goose, this is Striker. Have the bandits made it back to your location?"

Grimaldi came back five-by-five.

"Roger," Grimaldi replied. "A jet just flew over low, headed your way. Looks like a Lear."

"Stand by."

"Standing by, Sarge."

At the far end of the runway, above the ebony peaks of the pines, he saw the jet's navigation lights and its black silhouette. The covert Lear cleared the trees and dropped the last fifty feet, touching down with squealing protest from the landing gears.

Bolan signaled Grimaldi. "Mother Goose, start your engines."

"Roger. Powering up now."

The UH-60 Black Hawk that Grimaldi had flown

to Louisiana was located about two miles to the northwest in a large open area. Bolan had waited for the jet to land so the cacophonic shrieking of its engines would mask the sound of the helicopter powering up. Even from two miles away, in the stillness of the night, the sound of the helicopter would have been heard easily from inside the compound. And that could have complicated things.

The jet sailed down the runway, slowing, shooting past the hangar as the plane lost more momentum. It burned up three-quarters of the runway before decelerating to taxi speed. As the plane passed Bolan's position he got a good look at it. The jet was painted matte black, and it had no registry numbers that he could make out in the poor lighting. The NVGs didn't pick out any more than his naked eyes had.

The Lear came about and cruised back up the runway and taxied onto the apron. The ground guide walked the jet in to the center of the apron and signaled the pilot to shut down. The aircraft stopped, and two members of the ground crew ran under the wings and chocked the tires. A fuel truck rolled out of the hangar and stopped abreast of the plane, and more men went about the business of refueling the jet. The pilot didn't shut down the engines. This was obviously going to be a touch-and-go operation, staying on the ground long enough to pick up their passenger and take right back off again. The Jeep sped around the hangar, stopping near the plane as the hatch dropped to the tarmac.

Bolan raised a pair of compact field glasses to his eyes. He adjusted the focus ring and brought the scene on the tarmac into sharp relief. The lawyer,

who he'd recognized from Mannix's photos, got out
of the SUV on the driver's side, looking around the
area nervously as if he sensed somebody was watching who shouldn't be. Jock Macon appeared on the
other side of the vehicle and opened the rear door
on his side, helping a striking young woman to get
out. She couldn't have been more than eighteen
years old, the archetypal blond pom-pom girl wearing faded jeans and a purple sweatshirt. She shouldered a yellow nylon shoulder bag and seemed in
good spirits.

Together they walked out halfway between the
Jeep and the Lear and waited.

An older woman stormed off the Lear, lips moving angrily as she closed the gap between herself
and the men in front of her, unloading with a little
brimstone of her own on her two hapless targets.
Bolan had no idea who the woman was but decided
to refer to her as Grandma Spitfire until he had a
name to go with the fury. The lawyer stepped in and
took over negotiations, and it took a minute for him
to get the angry woman quiet enough so he could
make his points. They went back and forth until the
lawyer pulled a long blue rectangle of paper out of
his overcoat and handed it to the woman. A check?
Grandma Spitfire reacted as if she was looking at a
big number printed out on that blue note. The lawyer
took the check back and put a moderate sheaf of
papers into her hand to replace it. He went over the
document and handed her a pen.

It was some kind of contract, and if she didn't
sign, the check wouldn't be handed over. They went
back and forth some more, and Bolan wasn't sur-

prised when she finally capitulated, initialing all pages and signing the last on the hood of the Jeep. She slapped the contract back into the lawyer's hand along with the pen and waited for that check to rematerialize.

Bolan shifted his surveillance to the furious activity taking place around the Lear. The baggage truck was pulled next to the plane's fuselage, and several men were moving large, heavy crates out of the cargo hold and onto the two carts. Those crates were big enough to be weapons crates. The boxes could also contain drugs. Anything seemed possible with this bunch.

He shifted back to the scene on the tarmac. Grandma Spitfire grabbed and hugged Pom-Pom Girl. The two seemed genuinely glad to see each other. Grandma shedded some tears, then she had the girl by the hand, whirled around and practically dragged her back onto the Lear.

The hatch pulled back up and latched.

The fuel truck drove back to the hangar, and the ground crew finished emptying the cargo hold.

Bolan activated his radio.

"Mother Goose, get in the air and hold in place. Wait for my mark."

"Can do."

Two men unchocked the tires, and the jet wheeled back onto the runway. At the end of the runway, the jet pivoted again, lining up for takeoff. The turbines screamed louder and louder, the pilot let the brakes go and the black aircraft launched down the runway.

"Come on in, Mother Goose! Look for my strobe!"

"Roger that!"

Bolan stowed the binoculars and flicked on the IR strobe clipped to his assault vest.

Now it was all up to Jack Grimaldi.

7

Gump Residence,
Odessa, Texas

Detective Jack Gaines wasn't a native Texan. He'd
served with the homicide division of the San Francisco Police Department for eighteen years and decided to wind down his career in the land of the
Alamo. He was writing a novel about a controversial
cop in San Francisco hunting down a serial killer
who made Hannibal Lecter seem like an ascended
saint, if comparisons were to be drawn. His serial
killer was loosely based on the Sex Maniac killings
during the summer of '82. That fish got away. In
the book, the killer got his just deserts from the same
.44 revolver that Gaines carried: the original-issue
Smith & Wesson Model 29 .44 Magnum revolver
with a six-and-a-half-inch barrel. Gaines needed closure for the one that got away. Maybe the book
would give him the illusion of closure he needed.

Detective Tom Collins met him on the porch of
the house and said, "You're going to love this one.
It's a treasure trove of ideas for your book."

Gaines scowled and took off his black sunglasses.
"Marvelous."

Gaines stepped into the house. The living room was off the entryway, and the place looked as if it had been rifled clumsily in a spur-of-the-moment search for valuables. Fingerprint teams were all about the room dusting for evidence, and a couple of crime-scene photographers were taking pictures of the mess.

Gaines nodded to the group as he passed through to the kitchen. "Morning, boys."

Collins followed the big detective like a faithful pup.

The kitchen was the nexus of police activity. A photographer was taking pictures of the bodies from different angles while forensics took swabs, looking for crucial DNA samples. Gaines looked to his left, down at the forensics guy—Mitch was his name—working on the little girl's body. The kitchen table was blocking the detective's view so he stepped around. Mitch stood and finished bagging his samples.

A ragged line had been carved under her chin, and the small amount of splashed blood beneath the body couldn't have been all the girl bled. There'd be pints on the floor from a wound like that.

He noticed the rusty brown semicircles on the floor around the body as Mitch filled in the gaps.

"Yeah, they took her blood."

Gaines grunted.

"Judging by the bruises apparent around her ankles, I'd say the bastards held her upside down by her ankles over a bucket or something, sliced her throat open and bled her out like a pig."

Gaines looked at the boy's body nearby. Same cut throat, same lack of spilled blood around the body.

"Homer there was the only one they didn't bleed."

Gaines turned around and looked at the body taped in the chair in the center of the carnage. The old guy was grimacing in death, eyes frozen open and milky. In front of Homer was the body of his wife, naked, wrists tied behind, chest down on the kitchen table, her head draped over the other side. He could imagine all too vividly what poor Homer's last sights were.

"How'd he die?" Gaines asked.

Mitch shrugged. "Don't know yet. He probably had a heart attack being forced to watch his wife being savaged like that."

"Marvelous."

"Bleeding the victims and taking the blood would suggest that we have a possible cult crime here. What do you think, Jack?" Collins asked.

"Perhaps the victims were bled and the blood taken to send us barking down the wrong back alley, to cover the real motive behind this crime. I'm not playing the cult card until I've exhausted every other possible explanation."

The photographer flapped his free hand at Gaines, who stepped out of the way while the photographer took a clinical shot of the woman's battered body.

"Maybe I'll look into a possible cult connection on this. It'll free you up to chase down every other lead," Collins volunteered.

"You do that, Collins. Knock yourself out. Just don't try and turn this investigation into an episode of *The X-Files* or you just might become the next alien-abductee case to titillate the gullible.''

"Hey, Jack. I'll only go where the facts take me. The fact that these people were drained of blood and the blood removed from the scene would suggest that this isn't your run-of-the-mill sex killer.''

"None of them are run-of-the-mill, Collins,'' Gaines growled. "Each killer is unique, like an individual snowflake. There is no such thing as an average, baseline sex killer.''

Before the exchange could proceed further, an excited yell from the basement signaled the discovery of the evidence that would shift the focus of the investigation into darker nooks and crannies than mere killer satanic cults could explain.

"Hey! Hey, I've got something down here! Take a look at this!''

Gaines hit the stairs at a run.

Midland, Texas

THE TWO MEN IN BLACK were waiting for the skinhead leader at the concrete picnic table. Two identical black Chrysler sedans were parked in the lot in adjoining spaces. The skinhead leader parked his rusty Impala next to the two black cars and got out of the vehicle. He nodded at the two specters in black and looked around at the desolate landscape, suddenly feeling uneasy.

These guys always rubbed him that way.

The man in charge, the guy he always met, was seated on the concrete bench with a laptop deployed in front of him. The skinhead leader only knew him as Mr. Saracino. He'd never seen the guy who stood behind Mr. Saracino. Another one of Saracino's attack dogs, no doubt.

He strolled up to the picnic table, trying to exude cocksure confidence, but didn't quite manage it. He stood back a couple of paces and smiled.

"I got what you wanted, Mr. Saracino."

"I had so hoped that you wouldn't disappoint me, Mr. Biggs."

"I got the picture disk."

The skinhead held up the computer disk. Saracino motioned for him to give it up. The skinhead took a step forward, reached across and handed it to the blond man wearing the black suit and sunglasses. Saracino looked at the label—Pictures, West Texas—and looked up at the punk. The skinhead felt like a bug under a microscope. He smiled sheepishly.

"That's the disk you wanted, all right. I saw the picture."

"Ah, you saw it."

"Yeah, on his computer."

Saracino nodded and put the disk into the laptop's drive. He clicked on the Shortcut To Winfile icon and activated the A: drive on the window. A list of picture files scrolled down the screen. He randomly picked a file. Double clicking the mouse button opened the file with a picture viewer. The file showed Gump's daughter eating a hot dog on the hood of a huge green SUV. The horizon was brown and flat, and several pump jacks were captured in the background like rusty metal dinosaurs.

Saracino frowned.

He opened the pull-down file menu and selected Open. The program read the contents of the disk, and he clicked on a second picture file.

The image showed Gump's children squatting in the dirt, searching for flint arrowheads. The entire disk was full of family digital photography.

Mr. Saracino was still considered green by his seniors, still getting his legs under him. In the wake of this blithering mistake, he'd be looked upon as green for some time to come. The SENSOPS agent was objective enough to see the valuable lesson that this situation offered to teach. He took the offer and learned. He made a mental note to make a hard-and-fast rule about contract work in the future: he'd have to make sure that the contractors had at least an ounce of common sense, and the intelligence to use it.

Relying on the skinheads to do the brutal work had been a good choice when it came to deniability. Had the mission amounted to just the rape and murder of the Gumps, the skinheads would have scored like champs. Now he could see that retrieving the computer disk also meant that someone had to at least know how to use Windows to make sure that he was taking the right disk.

Another lesson learned.

Saracino looked up at the punk and smiled like a shark.

"So, you made sure that this was the correct disk before you left the house."

"Hey, I said I saw it on—"

"I know what you said."

Saracino's hand floated up and into his black suit

coat. The punk's eyes got big with realization, and he hopped backward while pawing to get hold of something stuck under his shirt in the waistband of his jeans.

Saracino palmed the Walther P-38, and a single stark gunshot cracked the morning calm. The punk's neck snapped back, and the top of his head erupted with a geyser of blood and bone. His body did a half backflip, following the ruptured skull to the dirt.

He spoke to the man behind him.

"Find the rest of his vermin and kill them. I don't care how you do it."

Gump Residence.
Odessa, Texas

"WELL, COLLINS, I think your satanic cult is looking more ridiculous all the time."

The four men were horseshoed around Homer's basement computer workstation, staring at the picture on the screen.

Collins furrowed his brows. "How do you figure?"

Gaines pointed at the screen. "Look at that helicopter. I'm no aviation buff, but I can honestly say I've never seen a helicopter that looks like that before. Look at these guys on the ground. Look at how they're dressed. How are they dressed, Collins?"

Collins squinted at the little black-clad figures on the ground in front of the hovering black gunship.

"They look like SWAT guys."

"Yeah, or some kind of crack military strike force."

"Okay."

"Work with me, Collins. We have a picture of a helicopter that nobody has ever seen before with a team of heavily armed commandos in the foreground. Do you think maybe that Homer took some pictures that he wasn't supposed to? Could these pictures have anything to do with this homicide?"

Collins saw a flaw with the theory. "Well, if they came to get these pictures, why didn't they take them?"

"Maybe they grabbed the wrong disk. Maybe they're a bunch of idiots. I don't know. Whatever happened, we have the disk now. How many pictures are on this disk, Elliot?"

Elliot Reid was a crime-scene technician and had made the computer discovery.

"There are three disks here. At least twenty-five, thirty shots. There's another one here you have to see."

Reid went to work on the computer, swapping out the disk in the A: drive with another disk. He scrolled to the picture file he wanted and clicked the mouse button twice.

The picture popped open and they were looking at a round metal ball with all kinds of tubes and wires hooked into it. The metal ball was inside some kind of smoky cowling, and the yellow-and-black symbol figuring prominently on the surface of the metal ball froze Gaines's blood.

"What the hell is this?"

"Judging from the pictures before and after this one," Reid said, "I'd say that this is a look inside the engine compartment on the wreckage of one of those helicopters.''

''Jesus.''

''That's a radiation warning, isn't it?'' Collins said. ''I don't get it. Was this thing carrying nukes?''

''That's the engine, Tom,'' Mitch the forensics guy said. ''This bird is apparently nuclear powered.''

''Tell me that satanic cults come equipped these days with nuclear-powered helicopters and I'll subpoena *The Twilight Zone*,'' Gaines said. ''Otherwise, I think we have our motive right here.''

''I think you'll be subpoenaing the CIA or worse over this, Jack,'' Reid told him. ''Looks like you get *The Twilight Zone* anyway.''

''Marvelous.''

Gaines stepped forward and popped the disk out of the tower. Two more disks lay on the desk next to the keyboard. The detective picked them up and put all three in his breast pocket.

''As the ranking man on this crime scene,'' he said, ''I'm ordering the three of you to complete secrecy over the existence of these disks. As of this second, they don't exist. We never found them. Those four people upstairs were tortured and slaughtered probably because of the pictures on these disks. If these people can do that, they won't even blink about rubbing out a few cops that know too much. That's the way it will stay until I can get these pictures analyzed and run some things down. Now, does anybody here now have any heartburn over this conspiracy I've just involved you in?''

He searched the faces of the men around him. Nobody spoke up.

"Okay, marvelous."

He turned to Collins. "Tom, I want this crime scene to spend all day, the next week, I don't care, cataloging and identifying every piece of evidence in this place. I want you to use any excuse to keep everybody busy. Whoever wanted those pictures is going to discover very soon that they've got the wrong disk, and I'm curious as to which federal agency it will be that will show up with some jurisdiction horseshit signed by a federal judge that will give them total control over our investigation. When the Feds show up, you call me, because I'm going to be at the lab getting these images analyzed."

Collins nodded, glad to be on the team again. "You got it, boss."

Upstairs the phone rang in the kitchen. It rang again. "Hey, somebody get that!" Gaines yelled.

There was a clomp of motorcycle boots on the linoleum, and the phone was picked up by one of the patrolmen up there. There was some conversation that Gaines couldn't make out, then the patrolman yelled down the stairwell, "Detective Gaines! I think you need to take this call, sir!"

"Who is it?"

"Some legal-acquisitions rep—a woman in Boulder, Colorado. Says she's calling for *Soldier of Fortune* magazine and wants to talk to the dead guy here."

"What?"

"Sir, this is officer shit. You need to talk to this woman."

Gaines trotted upstairs and took the phone from the patrolman.

"This is Detective Gaines, Odessa homicide. Who is this?"

"Did I dial the right number? Is this Homer Gump's residence?"

"Yes, it is. May I ask who's calling?"

"This is Lynzie Stremel. We received a picture and a letter over the Internet yesterday, and I'm following up on this."

"You're with *Soldier of Fortune* magazine, is that correct?"

"Yes, it is."

"Do you go by Ms. or Miss or Mrs., ma'am?"

"Oh, ah, 'Lynzie' is fine."

"Marvelous. I'm Jack."

"And you're a cop, Jack?"

"That's correct."

"What's going on? Where's Homer Gump?"

"Gump and his entire family were found brutally murdered this morning. Can I ask what Homer sent you?"

"My God…yes. He sent a cropped picture of a very strange-looking helicopter and a very alarming letter about the pictures he had taken of New World Order black helicopters in west Texas. My God, do you think that somebody killed them because of the pictures?"

"We can't comment on that. I've recovered Gump's picture disks. By some stroke of luck, the killers either took the wrong disk or missed them totally. I can personally attest to the very compromising nature of these photographs. I suggest you send your best reporter down here right away. Whatever the hell is going on down here, I think that our best weapon is exposure. I think these bastards are terrified of being exposed more than anything else."

"Do you think we're in danger here?"

"I think that you need to keep this extremely confidential. Is that understood?"

There was a worried silence on her end. "I understand. What should I tell Mr. Kirkland?"

"Tell him to send his best reporter. If you give me a vehicle to expose these people in, I'll open the books of this investigation to your writer. That would include sharing all the photographs with your magazine. Tell that to Mr. Kirkland. Do we have a deal?"

"Yes, I think we do."

"Great. Now get cracking. We may not have much time here, especially if they've got these phone lines bugged."

Lynzie Stremel abruptly hung up. The thought of bugs was unsettling, and he ordered Collins to have a line check done to answer that question.

Now he had to have the pictures looked at, one by one, and hopefully get an idea where the photos were taken. He had a lot of ground that needed to be covered quickly. Gaines put his wraparound shades back on and exited the house. Collins followed him out, just in case Gaines had any more last-minute instructions for him. Traffic was picking up around the murder scene. Neighbors in their robes and nighties were already out on the lawn, gawking. Patrolmen had put up a yellow crime-scene tape around the perimeter and were enforcing it.

A patrolman guarding the front saw Gaines and whistled.

"Detective Gaines! I need you over here!"

Gaines scowled and diverted from his car. A stocky, medium-height man dressed completely in black stood quietly in front of the patrolman. Gaines took the extra second to check the guy out. Blond. Wayfarer sunglasses. The guy would look FBI if he had on a white shirt instead of a black one.

The patrolman handed Gaines an ID wallet, and the detective flipped the wallet open.

He looked up at the blond man and smiled.

"Mr. Saracino with FEMA, is that correct?"

Only a federal agency could dress its people and send them out into the world looking like that.

The blond man nodded. "Yes, it is."

"What can I do for FEMA this early in the day?"

"My agency was activated in west Texas two days ago, Detective. You should have been informed at muster or roll call that all state and local authorities within west Texas were now taking their orders directly from FEMA."

"No, I honestly hadn't been informed of this change."

"Now you have been. I believe the laws in this matter give me all the jurisdiction I need to cross your police line."

"This is the scene of a brutal homicide. Four of them, in fact. I just can't see how there could be anything of interest to your agency at my crime scene."

"All right, Detective. I'll level with you. Your victim in there has been identified as sympathizing with extremist political positions. We have a situation in Big Spring right now that could represent a direct threat to the duly constituted civil authorities in the state of Texas."

"What kind of a threat?"

"A domestic terrorist threat."

"Homegrown—is that what you're saying?"

"A splinter group of the original Republic of Texas movement. They're ready to begin removing all government authority that doesn't recognize their declaration of Texas as an independent nation with force of arms."

"So they've got a militia."

"Yes."

"I didn't know that antiterrorism was being headed up by disaster relief these days."

"Our job is to provide continuity of government in the event of a national emergency. Disaster relief is something we do for PR when the locals can't find their asses with both hands."

"Really? Actually, I heard it the other way around, Mr. FEMA. I heard it that you were the guys who couldn't find their asses with both hands."

Saracino colored a little under Gaines's barb.

"Disaster relief isn't even part of our charter. Okay? We—"

"Yeah. Continuity of government in case the other one breaks. Right? We have a spare government in reserve. That's what you guys are all about."

Saracino was done being played with, subtly

milked for information. It was time to do a little milking of his own. A little more bluntly.

"Detective, I have all the jurisdiction I need to cross your line and take into custody any evidence I feel will assist me in completing my job here. Are you going to contest that?"

"No, but I would like to know what you're looking for."

Saracino studied the big homicide detective for several heartbeats, deciding how he should be answered.

"I'm looking for disks."

"Computer disks?"

"Yes, and any hardware that might be present."

"I can tell you that there is a top-of-the-line computer station in the basement and that there are a number of computer disks on the desk. I'll also tell you that looking through that material for evidence in our own investigation hasn't even begun yet. Perhaps that will save you some time."

"I'll fax you a report if I find anything that might be of assistance in your investigation."

"That's mighty generous of you."

Gaines turned to Collins with an update on his current instructions.

"Tom, I want you to be Mr.—" He flipped the wallet in his hand open for a refresher. "I want you to be this investigation's liaison with Mr. Saracino of FEMA. Full cooperation, Tom. This man is from the federal government."

Collins almost smirked. "You got it."

He turned back to the Fed and handed over the ID wallet.

"Thank you, Detective. I appreciate the cooperation."

"Just doing my part. And, Tom, you don't need to call me with that information anymore. I think all my questions have been answered."

Gaines strolled off back to his car, got in and drove away.

8

Midland, Texas

Bolan had an idea while en route from Barksdale AFB to Midland, Texas, riding second fiddle in an F-16 courtesy of the Louisiana Air National Guard. There were five more F-16s from the same squadron, flying in a V, carrying the Phoenix-Able contingent and the senator. They had managed to get in front of the Lear and would be on the ground with ten minutes to spare. Bolan radioed ahead for what he wanted: two sedans with U.S. government plates and six black suits, shirts and ties. With matching sunglasses.

The FAA guy in the tower at Midland-Odessa airfield gawked at the "suits" part of the request, but Bolan's presidential authority took the gawk out of the guy. Bolan had everyone radio in their suit sizes. They were going to be on the ground within forty minutes, so Midland tower had that long to cough up the requested items.

The sun was already up about ten degrees on the horizon. Daylight was burning.

When they touched down and taxied off the runway, Bolan saw one government-plated sedan parked and waiting for them, an anxious-looking FAA guy standing beside the car in his shirtsleeves, top button of his collar undone, tie unknotted. He looked a little stressed.

Bolan gave the guy as long as it took for him and his team to get out of the F-16s, retrieve their gear and assemble in an informal formation on the taxiway.

Still no sign of a second sedan or those six suits.

"Side arms and a good assault weapon as backup," Bolan told his men. "Stow everything else in the trunks when we get out of here. I'm going to find out where our other set of wheels are."

He stalked up to the wide-eyed FAA bureaucrat. "What's your name."

"Larry. Larry Johnson."

"Okay, Larry. Where's my other car? Where are those suits I wanted?"

"Ah, they're on their way here right now."

"You got a solid ETA?"

"Ah, soon. Very soon, I hope."

"Yeah. Me, too, Larry."

For Johnson's sake especially, the sound of squealing tires was pure music. He and Bolan both turned toward the source of the noise: another government-plated sedan was powering around the pylons holding up concourse A, horn blaring and accelerating across the taxiway, vectoring in directly on the waiting new arrivals and one relieved bureaucrat.

"Just a few minutes late. Sorry," Johnson said.

Bolan chuckled. "Not bad, Larry. You obviously know the talents of your people and put the most competent individual on the job. I'll mention that in my report."

"Thank you."

The second sedan screeched to a halt next to the first one, and a female ball of energy jumped out of the car yelling, "I've got the suits! I've got the suits!"

"Thank God."

Bolan pulled a wad of hundreds out of the left breast pocket of his blacksuit.

The woman was about five foot three in heels, brunette with her hair cut in a pseudo-Dorothy Hamill style that was longer and fuller, perfectly accentuating her china-doll face.

She stepped up to Bolan and looked up at him for approval. She blew a stray curl out of her face.

"Excellent work. What's the damage?"

"About three hundred and fifty dollars. Rounded up."

Bolan peeled off four C-notes. "That should cover everything."

He peeled off two more and handed them to the woman.

"What's this?"

"Job incentive. I appreciate your sense of urgency."

"Thank you..."

"Rance," Bolan lied.

"Rance. Oh, well, I guess you need those suits."

She went to the rear door on the car, opened it and draped the suits over her arms. She carried the clothing to Bolan and heaped it all in his arms.

"Thanks."

He walked back to his men and handed over the bundle. "Get your sizes, strip and get dressed. Make it fast."

That Lear was going to be flying in any minute.

Bolan was their leader, so he led by example. He unbuckled the assault vest and stowed it in his duffel. He unlaced and removed his combat boots, then unzipped the blacksuit and let it drop to his ankles. He was wearing woodland-camouflage-pattern boxer shorts and black wool Army-issue boot socks.

"Hey, look, guys," Schwarz said, "he's wearing the boxers I got him for Christmas three years ago. Rance, that's very touching."

They all dressed quickly, keeping their radios with them, and packed the rest of their battle gear into their duffels. Bolan was knotting his tie when he asked for the keys to both cars. He popped the trunks on both vehicles and told his men to load their gear. He gave the keys to the first car to Blancanales. Schwarz, his Able teammate and Grimaldi would take that vehicle, and Bolan, McCarter and the senator would ride in the other.

They rolled as soon as they were loaded.

From everything Bolan had seen and heard at Tranquillity Base, Mannix knew that the old woman and her granddaughter were two of his constituents. The media circus that the elderly Mrs. Horn had whipped up had broken out in pockets all over the country. The event caused Mannix to reassess just how much control COMCON actually had over the media. Otherwise, they should have squelched that story before it ever hit the papers. Then an anonymous jacket showed up on his desk one morning detailing some revealing background on the key players at Tranquillity Base, and the senator was ready to launch a fact-finding mission into northern Louisiana.

Mannix directed Bolan from the front seat on how to get to Cornelia van Horn's place from the airport. While the senator told Bolan where and when to turn, the soldier used a cell phone and called Information to be connected to the switchboard at Midland PD. While he was being put through to the commander of the patrol, he had Schwarz get Brognola on his cell. Bolan got the patrol commander's name and extension and had Brognola give the guy a call while he waited on hold. When the patrol commander came back on the line, he extended Bolan every courtesy.

Bolan told him what he wanted. With the senator's help, he detailed to the patrol commander how he wanted a police presence staying out of sight but creating a corridor from the airport to the Horn house that could be pulled tight to seal off the area on Bolan's command. They would funnel Kyler Applegate along that corridor, and when the girl and her grandmother were safely isolated in the house, they'd surround the area and take Kyler into custody before she could be activated to do whatever she was programmed to do.

He wanted the airport cops to watch for the Lear and identify how Horn and her granddaughter were being transported from the airport.

The patrol commander said "Uh-huh" a lot, making notes as Bolan listed the preparations. He assured Bolan that his request would be put into action immediately and broke the connection.

McCarter rode in the back seat, ready to use a 9 mm Uzi on either side of the car to lay down suppressive fire if the need arose.

The senator told the Executioner to slow down and take the next right. The car turned onto a residential street, lined with a row of older middle-class homes badly in need of some paint and a little yard work. The trees on the street were crackling with new spring growth.

Cornelia van Horn's house was the last one on the block, a one-story ranch with white vinyl siding. Cornelia's car, a fire-engine-red 1978 or '79 Firebird, was parked under the carport, nose to the street.

Bolan took a right at the corner without signaling. He made a radio call to car two as he did so.

"Pol, I want you to go through the intersection, go halfway down the next block and park. Keep an eye front and rear to what's coming."

"Roger."

Bolan braked and spun the wheel. The sedan switched curbs and stopped. The second sedan crossed the intersection in front of them.

"David, keep an eye on the rear," Bolan said.

McCarter nodded and watched the backtrack.

The Executioner settled back in his seat and watched the house. He didn't expect to be waiting long.

He just hoped that they could get the girl into custody and safely tucked away before her puppet masters were even aware that she'd been taken out of the play.

The cell phone vibrated in his pocket. He pulled the phone out and hit the send button.

"Pollock."

"Sir, Midland PD. I'm calling you with an update. Your corridor has been established and your suspects are en route in a steel-gray Lincoln limousine. ETA under ten. You're going to have to call me here when you want all units to converge on your location, and I'll relay the order to the troops."

"Excellent work, Midland PD. I want instant response time on this."

"You'll have it, sir."

Bolan ended the conversation and pocketed the cell phone.

So far, so good.

His FEMA ID SAID his name was Ronald Reichman, and the Midland chief of police, Alex Dale, didn't much care for him or the agency he worked for. Reichman and a small team of men had arrived in the evening two days earlier and announced that FEMA was on alert in west Texas. Midland was going to be their command center and from now until the "crisis" was officially declared over, orders would be flowing from the top down through FEMA. Which meant that Reichman was now Dale's boss.

The past two days had been an education for the chief; he had a greater appreciation of the Founding Fathers' suspicions of strong, centralized federal governments. If Thomas Jefferson or Thomas Paine could have sat in with Chief for the past two days and watched what FEMA was up to, they'd have probably been in the streets trying to incite a popular revolt.

The FEMA preparations for the possible "serious" emergency revolved around realigning all local civil and defense assets to operate under conditions of martial law. Army civil-affairs units and military-police battalions from all over the U.S. were being deployed throughout rural west Texas, setting up to step in and become the government during the crisis and enforce the state of martial law.

Reichman didn't talk a lot about the nature of the suspected emergency about to break, only that it was both terrorist and domestically organized. Dale deduced that the Feds were after militia people again. Well, if their expected militia activity took place and they immediately started trying to grab people's weapons, Dale knew that the militia enemy would become pretty much the whole population of west Texas. Texans like their guns.

Dale couldn't see how any of these preparations were going to defuse or divert a total catastrophe. FEMA's battle plan would only serve to exacerbate the situation with more guns going off, more skirmishes and more shoot-outs than Reichman and his men were going to be able to deal with. The Feds would have to carpet bomb the entire state to put an end to the revolt because once west Texas was under federal siege, the rest of the state would rally to join their countrymen in the fight to keep Texas free. Reichman didn't seem to show even trifling concern for the bomb he could set off here. By all appearances, he appeared to actually believe that order and control could be maintained while the population threw everything they had at him, lobbing every object that could possibly become a lethal projectile in the general direction of anyone looking like a gun-grabbing Fed.

The chief didn't think they'd be able to pull it off.

Hell, the bastards were shown the door in Florida in the wake of Hugo. If they couldn't even coordinate disaster relief, what in hell did they think they were going to do when total war broke out in Texas against FEMA?

Dale had to admit, though, that Reichman in his intimidating black suit, shirt and tie, seemed not only competent, but ruthlessly organized, as well. He and his spooks were a well-oiled tyranny-installation machine. They were all weaned on Machiavelli and Demig. Efficiency applied to the mechanics of oppression.

They were a scary bunch of bastards who should have worked for Nazi Germany or Stalinist Russia, not the U.S. government. Dale was still trying to get around the fact that the federal government even had an agency whose sole purpose was the continuation of government in the absence of the Constitution under martial law. It seemed so reprehensible and traitorous.

Traitor being the operative word here.

He was seated behind his desk doing a crossword puzzle when one of Reichman's spooks walked into the office without knocking. The man spoke to Reichman, who was seated on the couch, without seeming to be aware that the chief was in the room, too.

Reichman was leafing through the latest reports

from the field on their operational level of readiness. He finished reading the page he was on before looking up at his subordinate.

"Yes, Number One?"

"Somebody acting on presidential authority is diverting police units to cover an operation I haven't been made aware of. Is this something you have knowledge of, sir?"

Reichman tossed the report on the coffee table in front of him and sat up.

"No. What's going on?"

The black-clad spook briefed Reichman quickly on the location of the corridor and the address that was being staked out.

"Who is this somebody acting on presidential authority? Do you have a name?"

"A colonel named Pollock operating through the Justice Department."

"I'm not familiar with anyone named Pollock. We have ultimate jurisdiction here. See that the police units involved return to their assigned patrol sectors and get a few of our people to that address and find out more about this colonel. Take him into custody if necessary."

"Right away, sir."

The spook exited the office, closing the door behind him.

"Trouble?" the chief asked.

"Nothing that could possibly concern you."

Reichman pulled his SENSOPS-issue cell phone out of his jacket pocket, hit Send and keyed a number. He was calling his control for more information on this sudden wild card, Pollock.

Reichman lowered the phone.

"Chief Dale, I need some privacy right now. You don't have clearance to eavesdrop on this conversation. I'll let you know when you can have your office back. Thanks."

The chief nodded, took his crossword puzzle and left his office.

Yeah, he was nothing much more now than a gofer. If men like Reichman were the harbinger of things to come, Dale didn't like what was slithering down the pike to be born. It went so much against everything he was raised to believe as a good American.

He had some decisions and some phone calls of his own to make.

If the shit hit the fan, he had to know which side of the pasture he was going to park his allegiances in.

THE EXECUTIONER HELD the Beretta 93-R level across the roof of the car aimed directly at the woman's heart and told her coolly, "Just stay right there, miss. Don't come any closer than that."

The woman was blatantly dressed for distraction, which was the oldest trick in the book. He couldn't believe they were actually trying it.

About thirty seconds ago, McCarter had whistled an alert. Bolan and the senator turned in their seats to be momentarily stunned by the sight of a gorgeous woman jogging up the sidewalk from the rear.

She was a honey-blond amazon, all legs and lithe torso moving like a Thoroughbred. She was wearing a full-body stocking made out of a shimmery golden spandex with tank-top straps. Her shoulders were bare and taut with muscles. She had on a bright yellow cotton thong panty over the body stocking, and she was one hell of a traffic hazard. The woman had a black nylon fanny pack, turned around so that the zippered pouch was snug against her washboard tummy. Bolan was peripherally aware that she was wearing expensive designer running shoes and half socks, but it wasn't her feet that focused his attention.

It was those mesmerizing breasts—double-D cups that were barely held in check by her sports bra.

She jogged past the parked sedan with a pixie grin, fully aware of the effect she was having on its occupants.

She stopped on the sidewalk several paces in front of the sedan and bent over, apparently tying her shoes, bending with excruciating slowness.

McCarter cracked. ''Oh, my God! Bloody American women have no consciences! This is bloody torture by any other name!''

She straightened after a minute, turned and threw her head back and laughed. She put her hands on her hips and started to move toward the senator's open window.

That was when Bolan figured that more was going on here than malicious teasing. The woman was a walking distraction bomb designed to get in and go off close while guards were down.

He was out of the car and showing her the black muzzle of the Beretta before she'd taken two steps toward the vehicle. She froze and moved her hands away from the tummy pack. Carefully, she lowered her black shades and flashed Bolan green eyes that seemed more amused than startled or fearful.

"Whoa, big fella," she said, "I'm a friendly."

"I'll be the judge of that."

Bolan came around the car and approached her. "I'm going to reach out and unzip your tummy pouch."

"Gee, is this how you try to get dates?"

"I don't date."

"You going to throw me against the car? Frisk me up real good?"

"Just behave, okay?"

Bolan unzipped the tummy pack, reached inside and pulled out a stainless-steel Walther PPK/S, a computer disk and an energy bar. He backed away, holding the little pistol in his free hand.

"And what were you planning to do with this?"

"That's just my insurance."

"Insurance on what?"

"Insurance against Neanderthals that think my being dressed like this is a license to grope, grab and feel."

"Uh-huh."

Bolan wasn't buying it. This woman was more than just a flagrant tease on a morning trot.

"Can I put my hands down now? You've got my piece. I'm not here to bump you guys off."

"What *are* you here for?"

She looked at the senator and gave him the answer. "Hello, Senator Mannix. You've been wondering about the anonymous intelligence reports that have been showing up on your desk in the morning for the past few months. I'm your source. This computer disk is the best intel we have on the Tranquillity Base facility.''

She returned her attention to Bolan. ''That disk should make it very easy for a soldier like you to figure out what the priority targets should be in this scenario.''

''What makes you think I even know what the hell you're talking about?''

She grinned. ''You look like a Striker-minded guy.''

''And which alphabet-soup agency do you work for?''

''That's not important. I'm here to get that disk into your hands and to remind you that there are still some people in the intelligence community who are loyal to this country and to our oath.''

Bolan had to play this one on the gut, and it said that this outrageous woman was solid, that he could trust her. So he handed her the weapon and the energy bar.

''I'll hang on to the disk, then.''

She crossed her arms and laughed, the sunglasses perched on the tip of her nose.

''I love the camouflage job! It'll probably only work this once, but that's all you need, right? But your Puerto Rican buddy won't fool them for a New York second. There are no minorities in SENSOPS. Remember who you're dealing with here. The master race. So you might want to put that Latin Romeo under the seat or something if you want to maintain your confusion factor.''

Bolan looked at Mannix. ''What's your take on this, John?''

"I think the Good Lord moves in mysterious ways, and that this patriotic vixen here is a mighty important piece on this chessboard."

"God, Senator, I just love the way you talk about a woman."

Bolan holstered the Beretta and pocketed the computer disk.

"Thanks for the heads-up. I just hope for your sake that you're not one of them, setting us up for an ambush. I'll remind you that dishonor has a very heavy price tag attached."

"I'm not stupid."

"What about Kyler Applegate?" Mannix asked. "What are they going to use her for? Another school yard?"

"No. The target is the FEMA office downtown in the federal building."

The senator wasn't sure his ears were working correctly.

"They're going to bomb themselves?"

"They're going to bomb a bunch of clerks that process the blizzard of FEMA paperwork. None of the MIBs will be in the office when it happens."

The senator frowned at her acronym.

"Excuse me, MIBs?"

"Yeah. MIB—Men In Black. What you guys are trying to pass yourselves off as."

The senator cocked an eyebrow. "I see."

"Do you?" she asked. "Senator, you and these killer-elite types are here today because we maneuvered you here. There is no more time on the clock. This is the operation! If their plot succeeds today, by the end of the week the state of national emergency will be declared and FEMA will become the government. Martial law will be in force from coast to coast, and the Constitution will be suspended. Of course, we can't allow that. We needed a monkey wrench.''

She pointed to the three men. ''You guys.''

THEO SCHMITT WAS the operative assigned to check up on Pollock and determine jurisdiction in their overlapping operations. He had no idea that the house Pollock was trying to isolate with a police net belonged to the grandmother of the girl whose mission today was the pivot upon which everything else would turn. Schmitt had only been briefed on the information necessary for him to complete his assignment. It was a security protocol that professional spooks called compartmentalization. An overall operation was broken down into chunks, and individual cells of operatives were assigned each chunk and only told enough about their chunk to complete the mission. This practice insured that if one or more cells were compromised, interrogation and torture could only reveal information specific to those cells. The big picture would still remain unseen.

Schmitt had no idea what he was driving into.

He was driving an unmarked white Crown Victoria police cruiser. The center dash was a blinking and winking vortex of lights, knobs and digital readouts. It was a state-of-the-art tactical operations center shoehorned into the space of a milk crate. There was the police-band radio, a multifrequency scanner, a small keyboard and brownie-size monitor radio linked to the mainframes at headquarters to run licenses and plates through and see if any arrest warrants came back. The center console between the two front seats housed the cellular suite.

Schmitt turned off the busy boulevard and onto a residential street. He spotted the quarry immediately as he cruised to the next intersection. Standing in front of the white government car was a big, hard-looking man dressed like SENSOPS. He was with a woman on the sidewalk whose jogging outfit looked as if it had been sprayed on. There was a stop sign at the intersection, but Schmitt didn't see it. He rolled right through, and completely missed the second government sedan parked at the curb halfway up the block on his left flank. His eyes were fixated on the Day-Glo yellow thong the woman wore over her bodysuit.

He stopped in the street parallel to the other car, and two sets of hostile-looking eyes were tracking him from inside the vehicle. The other two were dressed in the same black suits. Who were these guys? They weren't part of his team.

He got out of the car, his eyes shifting from the guys in the car to the big guy standing near the woman. The big guy had the unmistakable aura of somebody who was in charge.

He didn't bother with introductions. There was protocol to be observed when operatives from different SENSOPS teams interfaced for the first time.

"Loyalty is honor," he said.

The big guy cracked a death's-head grin and replied, "You've got it all wrong, guy. It's 'Death before dishonor.'"

Schmitt's eyes bugged, and they both went for their concealed hardware at the same time.

The statuesque woman was already there, pointing a little silver pistol at Schmitt. He heard the first shot as the lights went out in his head.

FOR A SPLIT SECOND of confusion, the Executioner thought that she was shooting at him. But the MIB's head snapped back, not his. The small-caliber bullet punched a neat red hole in the guy's forehead, and he bounced off the open door behind him, pitching forward on rubber knees before going down face first into the asphalt. The body shuddered, then relaxed with a sigh.

Bolan touched his throat mike. "Stay in position, Pol. Shots have been fired, but the threat is neutralized."

"Everything cool?"

"Yeah. Hold in place until I call you in."

"Roger."

The Executioner regarded the woman as she tucked the Walther into her tummy pouch.

"Thanks, but I don't think I needed the help."

"Action talks," she said. "Now you know I'm a friendly."

"All I know is what my gut tells me. My gut tells me I can trust you. For now. But if you or your people ever set me up for a suck play or show me any duplicity whatsoever, I'll hunt you and all your buddies down like dogs."

McCarter was outside the car beside the corpse, going through the guy's pockets for anything useful. He pulled out an ID wallet and flipped it open.

"He's FEMA, all right."

The woman nodded her approval. "That's fair enough. Today's a pretty big day for this country. Don't let us down."

"I haven't failed my country yet."

"No, you haven't."

"In the future, if I need something quick, how do I contact you?"

She laughed. "I'm not giving my phone number out today, big boy. I'll contact you when we need your special touch of love."

"You got a name or should I just make something up?"

"Lauren Hunter."

The squeal of tires to his read sent the Executioner into combat mode. He dropped to a crouch and pivoted, palming the Beretta. McCarter had the Uzi shouldered and locked on. A white Gran Prix with smoky windows was sliding around the same corner Hunter had come jogging from.

"It's okay! They're mine!" she yelled.

The car braked in front of the unmarked cruiser and the driver revved the engine dramatically. The passenger-side door popped.

"That's my ride. Gotta go."

Hunter ran down the sidewalk, waving before she slid into the car and slammed the door behind her. The car backed up at full throttle as soon as the woman was in, then the driver slammed on the brakes and spun the wheel. The car pivoted in the intersection ninety degrees and took off like a cannonball for the boulevard.

"That driver certainly has a flair for the dramatic," McCarter commented.

"Spooks are a bunch of showboats," Bolan growled.

The Briton lightly kicked the corpse on the leg. "Not much more on him than his ID and a Walther P-38."

"A P-38? Why aren't I surprised? Park the car and the body in the alley behind the van Horn place. And keep that ID wallet."

McCarter nodded and went to work.

Bolan got back into the sedan and watched the house for the limousine.

"This is getting to be more tangled than a bowl of goddamned spaghetti," Mannix stated.

"Amen."

"That boy was technically a federal agent."

"I don't care what their day jobs are. They're cannibals, and I'm going to cut them down to the last guy."

Mannix chuckled. "That's the spirit."

The street-side rear door opened, and McCarter jumped back into the car. "They're calling for their mate on the radio."

"Did you answer?"

"No."

"They'll figure it out soon enough."

"Bloody right they will."

Bolan's earpiece crackled. It was Schwarz.

"Big limo just turned off the main drag. Coming our way."

"Roger," Bolan said, and pulled out the cell phone. He scrolled through the memory and hit the send button. The phone autodialed the number he wanted. The switchboard at Midland PD answered, and Bolan gave the woman the extension he needed. The limousine was a big Lincoln stretch, and it stopped at the curb in front of the Horn house. A blond MIB with sunglasses got out of the driver's side and went around the car to the curb.

Bolan was still waiting for the patrol commander to pick up.

"Dammit, come on!"

The patrol commander came on the line as the MIB opened the rear door of the limo and Cornelia van Horn emerged into the bright morning sunlight.

"I need that net thrown right now, Midland PD," Bolan said urgently.

The guy sounded reluctant to talk. "I'm, ah, sorry about this, sir. I've been ordered to reassign your units to their previous patrol sectors. We have a situation here, FEMA is calling the shots and—"

"Yeah, I know all about FEMA. Screw it. Thanks anyway."

He terminated the link and said, "We're on our own."

CORNELIA VAN HORN OPENED the door to Kyler's bedroom and stepped across the threshold. The muffled voice coming from behind the closed door had attracted her, and Kyler was following like a smiling pup.

"What in the name of Jesus?"

The redecorators had been busy while she was gone. The teenage girl's room had undergone several changes in the past seven hours. Her posters of

Pearl Jam, Jewel and Britney Spears were still on the walls, and her pastels of ponies and horses in sunny pastures, too, but now there were some additional posters hanging that were a left hook from an extreme right-wing field. One said Get U.S. Out Of The UN Now! There was a red circle and slash over the seal of the United Nations. Another said Support Your Local Militia and pictured Colonial Minutemen. A third poster was a cartoon depiction of King George III remarking to an American colonist holding a flintlock, "What use would a farmer have with a military assault rifle like that?" There was a picture of George Washington, Thomas Jefferson and Thomas Paine, as well as a lithographic reproduction of the Declaration of Independence, the Bill of Rights and the original Constitution of the Republic of Texas. Scattered about the floor and on the bed was a veritable library of mayhem: Army field manuals on guerrilla warfare, weapons marksmanship and demolitions, anarchist pamphlets and the *Poor Man's Atomic Bomb*. Also on the floor, at the foot of her frilly four poster, was an OD green crate with black stenciling on it. The crate was about as long as a rifle.

On Kyler's mirrored bureau was a small cassette player and a continuous loop tape was droning over and over in a monotone: "Call your operator. Code Alpha 3 Zulu."

The doomsday phrase that paid.

Cornelia was turning to say something to Kyler when the world exploded with a violent thud and her sight went white with orange nova bursts of light. The impact point had been just left of the base of her skull. The fact that she had been turning when the blow struck saved her from being killed instantly. The tough old woman was thrown forward into the white antique dresser, and her chin banged on the top of the dresser, scattering the knickknacks.

She was aware of Kyler stalking around on her right, falling on the green crate like a jungle cat on prey. Kyler was no longer interested in Cornelia. In Kyler's killer-elite mind, Cornelia was rose-bed fertilizer now. Her face was a twisted sneer of bestial blood lust. She attacked the metal latches on the crate, tossed the lid back and pulled out a black rifle with walnut-stained hardwood stocks, shiny with varnish.

Cornelia struggled to her feet and drunkenly tried to make it to the door.

THE MIB LIMO DRIVER MADE it to the sidewalk when the sound of a car engine maxing rpm and pealing away from the curb up the block snapped his head in that direction. Through smoky gray shades, the COMCON operative saw a white or gray sedan bearing down on the intersection. Somebody whistled loudly at him from his right rear, and he took the audio bait, turning in that direction.

Three very serious looking men walked toward him, radiating menace, coming from the street on the carport side of the house. The whistler was out front with the other two slightly to the rear, making a triangular wedge. All wore black sunglasses and the black suits of SENSOPS agents. The lead man, the biggest of the three, held a black pistol with a long sound suppressor against his right thigh. The man to the right held an Uzi at the ready, and his flanking sidekick held a huge silver handgun in front of him in a two-handed grip.

The sight was slightly off center and caused him to freeze with a flash of indecision.

"What's going on?" he asked lamely.

"We're scrapping this operation," the lead guy said in a graveyard voice.

"What's going on?" he repeated.

The Executioner brought up the 93-R so fast the move was a blur. He let the two 9 mm slugs shed some light on the guy's confusion.

The first low-velocity sizzler took the guy dead between the eyes and cracked the sunglasses in two at the nose. A lens and temple each flew into space, revealing big, rolling eyes with the light already gone in the irises. Round two shattered his cheek, and the guy crumpled to the sidewalk without making a sound.

Blancanales made a rocking stop parallel to the limo; both front doors and the rear door on the curb side of the sedan popped open as all hell broke loose from the front of the Horn residence. The long picture window exploded around the catapulting body of Cornelia van Horn, bucked off her feet and thrown backward through the glass by three high-velocity 7.62 mm rounds through the chest. Blood erupted from the exit wounds in her back like ugly flowers, misting the air around her flailing body. The old woman landed on the lawn and stayed still, sightless eyes staring into the glowing blue of the morning sky.

McCarter reacted like the superb soldier he was,

dropping to a knee and swinging the Uzi toward the window breech; he fired a precise burst into the house at the unseen assailant.

"Cease fire!" Bolan shouted.

He pivoted toward the three men still in the street. "Cover the front of the house. David, you're with me! We're going inside, and I want this girl alive!"

McCarter nodded, and he and Bolan sprinted for the front door. The Executioner knew that Kyler Applegate was essentially innocent in all of this. She hadn't asked to be made into a killer. She was a pawn, an expendable pawn on a suicide mission. Since seeing her briefly on the airfield in Louisiana, he'd been visited by the memory of another teenage girl who'd never had a chance to live the life the universe had given her. His sister.

The two Stony Man warriors hit the porch and flattened against the house to the left of the front door. They had their weapons ready.

"Let's stay low and go for a tackle."

"I'm following your lead, mate."

Bolan grabbed the screen-door handle with his free hand and opened the door. Bracing if against his shoulder, he grabbed the doorknob and shoved. He waited a couple heartbeats for a response, didn't get one and tensed to rush into the house.

The door near the carport opened with a loud crack, smacking into a wall or some kitchen cabinets. Schwarz yelled "She's going for the car! She's going for the car!" Then there was a hollow tin boom as the metal screen door was body slammed out of the way in an adrenaline-crazed exit. Three thundering reports from an assault rifle compelled

Schwarz and Blancanales to duck behind the hood of their car for cover.

To Bolan's educated ear, the weapon sounded like something Soviet: an AK or SKS. The Stony Man warriors in the street returned fire with three short bursts. McCarter had dropped to a crouch and was duck-walking quickly along the front of the house, moving on the carport. The Executioner rushed into the house, sprinting through the living room, side-stepping a formal dining table and continuing into the kitchen, angling for the open exit.

A car door slammed shut, and a throaty V-8 engine roared to life.

Bolan caught her profile inside the car and he raised the Beretta to fire. The girl yanked the Firebird into Drive, stomping the gas pedal to the floor. His hasty shot impacted on the rear windshield, shattering it as the car pounced forward like a ground-bound projectile out of the carport and into the street, Stony Man weapons barking in opposition to the gutsy charge. Bolan heard the Firebird's headlight lenses popping and the front end getting chewed by multiple bullet strikes.

He straight-armed through the screen door and outside.

Kyler wasn't one for fancy wheel work. She gunned the Firebird straight out the driveway, across the street and jumped the curb on the other side, making a break for the boulevard, spinning tires clawing up grass and dirt as the tail wagged recklessly.

Schwarz, Blancanales, Grimaldi and McCarter piled into the second sedan, and the car shot off down the street, paralleling the Firebird weaving around trees. Bolan broke and ran for his car, hearing the senator's boots pounding turf behind him.

Steam and smoke curled from the Firebird's hood. The radiator had to have been perforated from the beating the front end of the car took from the volley of shots. With any luck, the engine would seize up long before the girl got anywhere near the federal building and her designated target.

The chase was on.

9

Detective Jack Gaines turned the problem over in his mind as he drove. He hadn't voiced his concerns at the crime scene because he didn't want to encourage Collins's streak of sensationalism, but it was the one fact in all this lunacy that didn't add up.

Why in the name of Zeus did the perps bleed them and take the blood?

Everything else added up. Gump saw something he shouldn't have and took pictures of it, which made silencing him mandatory in the world of cloak-and-dagger secret ops. Yet if the Gumps were dead because they had seen some sort of prototypes for future military aircraft, the crime scene he'd just observed didn't fit that scenario at all. If the spooks had come to get them, he'd figure on finding the whole family neatly laid out like cordwood, double-tapped in the back of the head execution style—not the Creature Features he'd just seen.

But...

If the operation that the Gumps had run afoul of was black enough, Gaines supposed that anything was possible. Hiring the most cranked-up acid-fed psychos this side of Charlie Manson to handle the loose ends for the spooks would make vicious sense when it came to deniability. The magnitude of the violence used against the Gumps and their children would draw the news magazine producers like vultures to carrion, and the focus would be on the seeming satanic nature of the crimes. The intelligence connections would be missed by all but the most ardent investigators. Guys like Jack Gaines. He had an edge that investigative journalists didn't—a badge and a .44 Magnum Smith & Wesson Model 29.

A small consolation when pitted against a monolithic Goliath with the resources that the CIA and their pedigree could wield.

What rankled the detective the most was the fact that the perps had bared their victims' throats over a bucket, sliced open both jugulars and most of the esophagus, then waited for all the blood that was going to drain to spill into their buckets so they could take it with them. What he couldn't decide for lack of information was whether the act had been committed so that the cops would be chasing down blind leads that would lead exactly nowhere, or if the perps bled the Gumps so that the blood could be used in something foul, dark and concealed.

He flip-flopped back and forth, trying to get a gut reading on which of the alternatives was the better of the two, brooding while he drove in light traffic on the Loop, a four-lane expressway that circled the Midland metropolitan area. Gaines was headed downtown to see a friend on the Midland force who could be trusted and have a look at all the picture files from Gump's disks on Midland's superior image-processing equipment.

His thoughts were broken by the call over the radio for an all-units response: shots had been fired and medical assistance was needed on the scene. Two people were down, and the suspects had fled the scene in two white four-door sedans. A third suspect and possible victim was driving a red Firebird, and the shooters appeared to be in pursuit.

Gaines noted that he'd just passed through the section of Midland where all the action was going down. He began to regularly scan his rearview mirror. If the chase spilled into his lap, he'd do something about it.

As he passed a shopping plaza on the right, he glanced into the rearview mirror again and saw the red Firebird slide out from behind a big royal-blue SUV three cars back. The Firebird gunned around the SUV and yanked back over into the opposite lane. It accelerated up the open lane, overtaking and rocketing past two more cars. The two chase cars appeared in the mirror, the lead car powering out in front of the SUV and changing lanes, letting the trailing vehicle take point.

Gaines reached inside his suit coat and pulled out his big-bore revolver, laying the cannon next to him. He powered down both front-door windows just in case he needed to shoot at somebody through either. He let the red Firebird roar by on the right, and saw that the driver was a pretty blond teenage girl whose face was a mask of crazed exhilaration. He let his foot off the gas, briefly coasting, letting the first chase car catch up. Then he flicked on the little bubble flasher mounted on the dash and jerked the big car in front of the first white sedan, goosing the brakes. The white sedan instantly darted out from behind Gaines and tried to accelerate away. The detective stomped the gas and stayed abreast of the shooter's car.

He hefted the Model 29 revolver and pointed it out his window at the guy riding shotgun in the car next to him.

"Police officer!" he yelled over the scream of the dueling V-8 engines. "Pull over or I'll shoot!"

Two guys were in the lead chase car. The guy behind the wheel glanced across at Gaines menacingly. He looked like a stone-cold killer. His partner looked too much like Texas Senator John Mannix to be believed—the same longish gray hair and walrus mustache, but this look-alike was wearing gangster shades and black attire that he'd seen on another fellow earlier, that FEMA agent.

The senator look-alike leaned out his window and yelled back, "You've got this all backward, boy! That girl is the one you need to be pointin' that gun at!"

Gaines's mind flashed back to that look on the girl's face and he wondered.

"You look an awful lot like a certain senator from the good state of Texas. Boy."

"No offense, Detective, but I'm John Mannix! That girl is a bomb, and she's set to go off downtown at the federal building! I'm here with members of the Justice Department putting a stop to this lunacy before something really bad happens."

The second sedan was on his rear now, crowding

the rearview mirror. Two guys in black suits and shades were hanging out the rear windows on both sides of the car, training black submachine guns on Gaines's head through the rear windshield.

"I think you've got your federal agencies mixed up, Senator! Aren't you working with FEMA here, not the Justice Department?"

The big menacing guy driving the chase car yelled over the engines and wind, "It's camouflage. Now back off, because we aren't pulling over."

"Marvelous."

The big guy gunned out in front of him, and Gaines let him do it. The trail car swerved around him and joined the leader. Gaines had a raging gut feeling right then that whatever was going down here was somehow connected to the massacre of the Gumps. He was going to tag right along on this to see where it led him.

Gaines pressed the pedal to the metal, and the car surged forward, eating up the separation.

THE TRAFFIC LIGHT ahead blinked from green to yellow. The red Firebird kicked it and found an extra hidden reserve of horsepower somewhere in that high-performance engine, redlining the rpm. The Firebird blasted through the intersection like a cannonball as the light turned red, and on the other side, the engine couldn't take the heat anymore. A teeth-rattling boom erupted from inside the engine, and the hood was punched from underneath by an invisible fist that domed the metal. A louder explosion followed, and the hood flew off into space on a column of fire, cartwheeling over the top of the doomed car and touching down in the intersection with a spark-showering clatter. Cross traffic in both directions screeched to a halt in the wake of the spectacular flame-out, which the two white government-plated sedans took advantage of. Both cars ran the red light without slowing, and a third car with a cop light in the window followed them through.

The Firebird zigzagged crazily, and Kyler shifted into neutral, letting the heavy car's momentum jump the curb. She steered down a short embankment and bounced into the parking lot of a shopping mall. The only cars in the parking lot belonged to the employees of Neiman Marcus, and the vehicles were parked in the back forty, leaving everything close to the store for the battalions of shoppers who would be descending on the store for the 9:00 a.m. kickoff of the spring green-apple sale. The Neiman Marcus store was an add-on, and it looked like one.

The architects who had designed the structure couldn't have been conscious of the mall they were fusing to; the Neiman Marcus monolith was like a Babylonian ziggurat of blocky, marble-faced opulence with entrances on three sides that were towering walls of glass and glitz. In contrast, the mall was an oasis of chrome, neon and earth tones. High Atlantis met the Anasazi across the gulf of time in the land of the Alamo.

The heavily damaged Firebird zeroed in on the closest of the three Neiman Marcus entryways.

The out-of-control car totaled the entire cosmetics department straight up the middle and finally came to a stop in the bordering hosiery-and-handbags department.

While the glass was still flying, slicing to ribbons all merchandise within range, three cars slid to a stop outside the jagged hole, creating a cordon. Doors popped open while the cars were still rocking on the shocks, and five dangerous-looking men dressed in black fanned out in front of the breach and prepped automatic weapons for the business of killing. A sixth guy joined the black-suited gunslingers. He was dressed in the usual professional attire—herringbone sport coat with suede elbow pads, charcoal-colored wool-blend trousers, a white oxford shirt and blue paisley tie. He wore black wraparound sunglasses and held a long-barreled handgun at his side. This guy was as big and as tall as the leader of the black suits, who stood at the center of the formation, his gunners flanking him on the right and left.

The Executioner racked a round into the pipe of the MP-5 and said, "No noncombatant casualties. I want the girl alive, but if she has to be taken out to prevent innocents from being harmed, then that's the way it's going to be."

The Stony Man warriors nodded their understanding.

Bolan eyed the stoic detective standing with his men, revolver in hand.

"Are you tagging along on this, Detective, or are you still trying to arrest us?"

"I'm pursuing a lead on a very ugly case."

Bolan said, "All right, then. Let's do it."

The Executioner took point, and his men fell into a V-shaped wedge around him. McCarter and Grimaldi took the right flank, Schwarz and Blancanales the left. The senator and the big detective stayed in the center of the wedge, several paces behind Bolan. They trotted through the swath of destruction with their weapons leading the way, scanning for the target.

As the group crunched through the wreckage of the cosmetics department, Mannix saw a bleeding and lacerated woman struggling to get out from under the ruins of a display case that had collapsed on top of her. He broke away from the fire team and went to help the woman free herself.

The red Firebird was buried up to the hood in broken plywood, glass and packages of Hanes control-top panty hose. The driver's-side door was open; the car was empty. Between the eye-tearing acrid smoke wafting from the front end of the car and the gagging sweet stench of perfume, there wasn't much clean air left over for breathing purposes.

A young man wearing stylish tortoiseshell glasses poked his head above the sales counter in women's accessories and shouted, "I called the cops! The cops are on their way!"

Three rapid-fire rifle blasts echoed like doom across the cavernous store, booming to the front. The young man ducked behind the sales counter. Bolan and his men took off at a dead sprint. Gaines yelled over at the cowering clerk, "Keep your head down if you want to keep it! We are the police!"

Then he took off after the black suits, his .44 Magnum pistol held out and ready.

THE NEIMAN MARCUS EXIT into the mall was as big as a hangar door. The metal-louvered fire barrier was rolled up halfway, allowing employees to go back and forth between the store and the food court in the mall. Several of the food vendors were already open, catering to the mall employees and the Midland Mall Crawlers, a group of senior citizens who walked the mall every morning before opening with handheld weights and garishly colored sweatsuits. The dozen or so food venders were located on a promenade that ringed a lower-level center court that was devoted to seating and public rest rooms. There was a huge fountain in the center of the dining area with a tile-walled octagonal pool.

The two dozen or so mix of workers and senior citizens were murmuring and milling toward the Neiman Marcus store, trying to figure out what was going on. It sounded as if an asteroid had just taken out half the building, and they could see smoke in there, which wasn't a good sign.

A running figure appeared out of the smoky murk, weaving around clothing racks and mannequins. The figure hit the polished black marble of the main aisle and sprinted toward the goggling crowd gathering in center court. Eyes flared wide and panic seized the locals as the blond girl in jeans, sneakers and purple sweatshirt ran out under the half-raised fire barrier into the target-rich environment of the food court. She was toting an AK-47 assault rifle, and a heavy-looking green canvas satchel bounced against her hip on a green web strap that was looped over the opposite shoulder.

She skidded to a stop at the railing above the center court and shouldered the rifle.

Pandemonium broke out below in the center-court seating area as everyone scrambled to keep from being the first target. The mall workers were young and fast; the mall crawlers weren't so spry anymore. It was a free-for-all brawl for survival—the weak were pummeled, clawed and kicked as those with the finely honed self-preservation instinct threw all sense of community out the window, overturning tables and anyone else who got in the way of the stairs up and out of there.

Kyler looked down upon the melee and laughed like someone over the edge; to stand there with the power to reduce these pathetic weaklings to their lowest common denominators by doing nothing more than shouldering a rifle was as heady as a narcotic.

The teenager let the crowd spread and selected her prey from the ones left behind.

One of the mall crawlers, a portly blue-haired woman with a hot pink running suit was intent upon getting her breakfast out of harm's way with her.

Kyler lined her sights on the woman's back. She had selected her first target.

The rifle boomed, and the front of the woman's running suit exploded like a balloon full of blood and muscle. Her corpse was sledgehammered face-first over the table, scattering chairs and food.

Kyler shifted, firing her next round across the food plaza and blowing the top of a luckless mall worker's head off.

For her third shot, she dropped her sight picture down and to the right. She held her breath on the exhale and squeezed the trigger. The 7.62 mm full-metal-jacket slug took the young woman halfway up the stairs square between the shoulder blades. The bullet exited the base of her throat relatively unde-formed and splattered the kidney of the man clawing to get around people in front of him.

Kyler vaulted the railing and dropped into the lower-level center court like a fleet reptile. She held the AK vertical on her firing shoulder by the pistol grip as she weaved around tables and debris.

She leaped up on the red-tiled wall of the fountain and spun around, the fountain jets shooting up ma-jestically behind her, and looked for someone else to kill. Her eyes froze on the men standing at the railing she'd just vaulted—five men in black and one big guy who was color coordinated. All of the men were pointing weapons at her, and there was no way she could take them all.

"Drop it," one of them shouted.

She laughed and brought the rifle to her shoulder and fired.

The Executioner beat her there and fired a single 9 mm round that hammered into the girl's firing shoulder like a baseball bat. She did a pirouette to her knees, managing to keep from being tossed over into the fountain pool, but the AK took a swim.

The girl panted, and her brain was momentarily scrambled by the pain and the shock.

What to do next. What to do next.

Her programming reasserted itself like a cold wash coming over her and turned down the neural volume on the pain, delayed the effects of shock. She laughed triumphantly. She stood, brought the green satchel to her chest and yanked out the black ring that kept the timed reaction from decaying.

"Satchel charge!" McCarter yelled. He fired a burst from the Uzi, and Kyler Applegate's purple sweatshirt was ventilated with bloody bullet holes. The girl was dead before she hit the water.

"Everybody down!" Bolan shouted.

Bolan and his crew hit the deck, covering their heads with their arms. Nobody remained in the center court but the dead. The satchel charge detonated as Kyler's corpse broke the surface of the water. Three sides of the octagon closest to the blast center were pulverized and cannonballed across that side of the center court, blowing tables to splinters and twisting the tube-metal seats into modern art. The water in the pool basin was heaved into the air in one mass, tainted rosy pink, and shot like a hydro-bomb through the glass dome above. The concussion shattered display windows up and down the branching corridors of the mall, and the entire building rang like a gong with noise that bloodied eardrums.

Bolan got to his feet, drenched and battered, working his jaw to quell the ringing in his ears. It was raining steadily in the food court now as all that water came back to earth. He started to checking his men, still in the prone position. Schwarz rolled over and smiled blissfully as Bolan squatted next to him.

"Groovy travel junkets you throw together, man."

Blancanales, McCarter and Grimaldi stood and shook it off.

"Everybody okay?" he asked. Everyone nodded and gave him the thumbs-up.

Bolan stepped over to McCarter. "Nice job."

"Don't mention it, mate."

The big detective sauntered over to Bolan and said, "So I take it that anywhere you guys go, you leave major chunks of real estate in smoking ruins."

"Usually we confine the damage to enemy turf."

"This one just spilled over."

"You could say that."

"I have a lot of questions."

"And I don't have the time. We're not done yet."

"No, not by a long shot," Gaines said.

Mannix wandered onto the promenade, awestruck by the scene of destruction. All he could say was "Oh, hell no."

Bolan rallied the Stony Man commandos. "We need to get out of here!"

The men in black beat a hasty retreat, jogging back through the devastated Neiman Marcus store. That green-apple sale wouldn't be going off today.

Gaines jogged with Bolan, refusing to let a dead dog lie. "What's going on around here?"

"There's a foreign element, descended from Nazi Germany, that's working from inside our government to suspend our way of life," Bolan told him.

"What do nuclear-powered black helicopters and FEMA have to do with this?"

Bolan stopped and faced the detective.

"What do you know about that?"

Gaines pulled several computer disks from inside his jacket.

"I took these from a crime scene this morning. Some very interesting photography."

Someone had been madly snapping pictures of the carnage in the wake of the ambush outside Big Spring, and it looked as if that person had a digital camera.

"The person who took these pictures, Homer Gump, was murdered, along with his family. By some stroke of luck, I think whoever did it took the wrong disks."

"They killed Gump and his family."

"They didn't just kill them. They bled the Gumps like pigs and took the blood."

Bolan gritted his teeth in anger. "Thanks for the intel," he said coldly. "Be careful with those disks."

Then he turned and sprinted after his comrades in arms, leaving Gaines standing there with a lot to think about.

CHIEF DALE READ in the FEMA agent's face that the news was unexpected.

The guy pocketed his cell phone, settled back into the cushions of the sofa and looked at the ceiling for several heartbeats, frozen in thought or disbelief.

"Problems?" Dale asked.

The FEMA man looked at him blankly, then smiled weakly.

"The emergency is over. I guess you get your office back, Chief."

"That's a damned shame."

"My men and I will be gone within the hour. I

officially place west Texas back under local control.''

''I'm glad you didn't have to do your job today.''

Reichman grunted and stood.

''Other emergencies will arise,'' he said cryptically, and stepped out of the chief's office and walked down the bustling corridor toward the elevators.

He pulled his cell phone out and dialed a broadcast pager number.

Out in the desert of west Texas, all over the oil fields, the fifty-six two-man direct-action teams culled from the First Texas Republican Militia's most hard-core members reached for their pagers at the same time, snatching the buzzing boxes off belts and out of pockets to peer at the message display.

Every one of those men fully expected to see the signal to initiate the operation.

The code was three digits long: ''666.''

Mission Aborted.

10

Tranquillity Base,
Northern Louisiana

Joe Newport didn't know what it was like to run for his life. He'd never had to do it before. He was much more comfortable with making other people run for theirs. They never got much of a start at it, though. They never saw Newport coming, which was a lot like this bastard, Bolan.

Newport hadn't see the son of a bitch coming.

The FEMA agent had applied pressure, but the President wouldn't give the guy up. A CIA contact told Newport there had been rumblings in the past that Mack Bolan, the Executioner, wasn't dead at all, but did freelance work for the Man.

He knew Bolan's reputation—had heard some unbelievable stories—but the Bolan Effect could never really be understood until it was experienced. Few people had survived a Bolan attack. All Newport could think about was escape as rockets, bombs and fireballs rocked the airfield around him. He had weaved through the burned-out skeleton of the maintenance hangar, heading for the rear door and the sanctuary of the tree line beyond.

Newport was receiving a painful education in the Bolan M.O. The man had dropped from sight in Texas two days ago after wrecking what should have been a simple snatch mission, destroying two multimillion dollar secret aircraft in the process, then surfaced again here in the wee hours of the morning, compromising their security system and killing a guard before making a daring escape right in front of everybody's eyes by helicopter. By breakfast, the bastard was in Midland derailing the best excuse COMCON had to date in justifying the declaration of a national emergency and seeing all its careful planning amount to nothing. And now, not even being suppertime yet, Bolan was back in Louisiana, and this time he wasn't alone.

Providing Joe Newport lived to see the next sunrise, he would never again underestimate this bastard's knack for hitting targets with lightning speed separated by hundreds of miles. Obviously, when this guy was in rampage mode, he didn't take time out for things like sleep.

A squadron of Apache gunships had appeared out of nowhere, hosing down the airfield with cannon and rocket fire, prepping the LZ for the invasion force that was surely right behind them. The attack couldn't have come at a more awkward time. The Committee had ordered Tranquillity Base shut down in the wake of Bolan's surprise morning visit. The potential now for exposure on this front was too great. The site was to be stripped of all sensitive equipment and sanitized, nothing left behind for inquiring minds to gawk over. The aboveground facility wasn't the problem. It was Aquarius's underground hole that was turning out to be a logistical nightmare. Everything had to be stripped out and hauled to the surface via one elevator shaft to the airfield where C-130s had been landing, loading and taking off all day long bound for their secure installation inside Nevada's Area 51.

Two C-130s were sitting on the apron being loaded when the attack commenced. The Apaches didn't fire on the C-130, but anything else on the airfield was fair game. After a thirty-second fusillade of rocket and electric-cannon fire directed at the trucks and ground personnel, the Apaches swarmed around the C-130s and made it very clear that those planes were going nowhere. Then the invasion force flew in over the southern tree line—a UH-60 Black Hawk leading three CH-47 Chinooks. The Chinook trailing left broke away from the formation and dropped over the apron at a fifty-foot hover. Two thick ropes snaked out the side door and off the rear ramp, and in about ten seconds what seemed to be an entire platoon of heavily armed infantrymen was deployed to the ground, surrounding the C-130s and taking prisoners.

The Black Hawk and remaining Chinooks continued their flight paths across the airfield and disappeared over the trees on the opposite side, heading for the administration building, the detention compound and the security bunker that led to Aquarius's laboratory of mind control and drug processing.

Newport made it into the trees as the helicopters carrying the assault force roared by overhead like avenging angels of death. He worked his way around to a good concealed vantage point that allowed him to get a spying eye on the troops taking down the airfield.

The air was heavy with humidity, and he was soaked with sweat. He took off his suit jacket and racked it over his arm. The troops were dressed in woodland BDUs, jungle boots, assault vests and Kevlar battle helmets. Their faces were painted with light-green-and-loam camou paint, in the same tiger-stripe pattern. The only troops carrying rucksacks were the ammo bearers on the M-60 crews. The rest of the soldiers carried M-16 A-2 rifles, some with M-203 grenade launchers mounted under the barrel, or M-249 Squad Automatic Weapons. He squinted, trying to focus on their shoulder patches.

Yes, they were wearing scrolls on the left shoulder—U.S. Army Rangers, the world-renowned experts at commando raids and airfield seizures.

Once Newport had learned just who this Pollock character really was, he'd used his top secret security clearance to pull the official jacket on one Mack Bolan.

He discovered that they had a human wolverine by the tail here, and if they couldn't get positive control of this guy, neutralize him ASAP, he was going to chew up the Fourth Reich and spit out the bones just like he'd done to countless others.

Newport had to pull the plug on this. In the course of a few hellish days, that son of a bitch was making him look like an incompetent, and that was a humiliation he couldn't bear. His flawless reputation was on the line. This was personal now. If it was the last thing Joe Newport ever did, he was going to be the man who ended Mack Bolan's reign of terror once and for all.

He'd bring in that bastard's head on a silver platter or he'd die trying.

With that promise in mind, Newport headed east through the tangle of the woods, toward the fence line and escape.

This battle was lost, but the war was far from over.

THE CHINOOK AIRBUS and Grimaldi's Black Hawk circled overhead like vultures. There was a battle of the bullhorns going on in the administrative parking lot between the Third Platoon leader, Richard Ecklebarger, and the Madison County sheriff, Bat Clevenger. The sheriff, his boys and their squad cars were cordoning off the entrance to Tranquillity Base from the county road. The deputies were behind their hoods, peeking over with riot shotguns trained on the Rangers, who squatted behind hoods of their own, setting up fields of fire that would chew those county boys worse than a bag full of meat-hungry wolverines.

The county boys were outgunned five to one. In terms of ammunition and firepower, if the order to open fire was given, they'd be yesterday's news. Instantly.

Ecklebarger repeated, "This is a United States military operation! We are United States Army Rangers. We are acting on the personal orders of the President of the United States. I say again—if you fire upon us or interfere in any way, we will stop you. Is that clear enough for you, Sheriff Clevenger?''

''You don't get it, soldier boy! My men and I are already actin' on federal orders! And just between you and me, the President doesn't have any jurisdiction in Madison County!''

Mack Bolan approached the first lieutenant and relieved him of the bullhorn.

''Sheriff, this is Colonel Pollock. I'm in charge of this operation. Your orders have been revoked. FEMA is no longer calling the shots here. I am. You can either act as our front guard for this operation, or we can take you into custody and process you as prisoners of war.''

''The hell you will!''

The sheriff let go of the bullhorn and yanked his service revolver from his holster, dropping to a crouch and aiming the weapon across the hood of the squad car.

''Shoot these Nazi bastards!'' he roared.

Clevenger opened fire first, and the shotguns followed. The chain-link front gate and fence were between the dueling parties, as well as fifty-plus yards of space. The scatterguns were instantly removed from the equation in respect to producing any casualties, leaving Sheriff Clevenger and his six-shooter their sole hope in drawing any kind of first blood.

The Rangers were behind their cover cars with the first shot from the sheriff's .38; Bolan sought cover, too, and silently congratulated these troops on their fire discipline. The order to return fire hadn't been given. They were holding in place until it was given.

Bolan needed to give the sheriff something to think about. He activated his throat mike.

"Jack, I need a couple of those Apaches now! I want them to fire a couple rockets each right over the top of those county mounties' heads into the tree line behind them—make that fifty yards in for safety's sake. How copy?"

"You got it. A few warning shots across the bow, coming right up."

The air throbbed suddenly as the two Apaches soared in low from behind, a single rocket pod on each fin of the birds hissing smoke and fire; the four whizzers flew over the cops almost too close for comfort. Close enough, anyway, to scare the deputies, robbing them completely of the will to do anything but reach for the sky.

The four rockets detonated exactly fifty yards into the tree line, doing the work of a crew of lumberjacks in under a second.

Once again, peace had been achieved through superior firepower.

Squad leaders were barking orders now, and two squads of Rangers rushed the front gate, M-16s and M-249s trained on the Madison County law-enforcement contingent. One soldier entered in the guard house and opened the front gate. The Rangers swamped the six county mounties and buttstroked them to the ground. Then the local law officers were handcuffed and taken into custody.

Bolan looked at the first lieutenant and grinned.

"We need to have a talk about unnecessary roughness, Lieutenant."

"One man's rough is another man's restrained, sir."

"Good answer, Lieutenant."

"Lieutenant, there are several teenagers in an underground lab facility who are victims of the people we're putting out of business today. I want the teens we find separated into one group, and I want them under constant surveillance until they can be evacuated and placed in the care of specialists. Is that clear, Lieutenant?"

"Yes, sir."

"Make it happen."

Lieutenant Ecklebarger yelled for his second squad leader, sergeant Blaine Acosta, who bolted from behind cover and double-timed across the lot to the lieutenant, dropping down next to him. Ecklebarger explained what needed to happen. The squad leader repeated his instructions to the lieutenant, then ran back to his position. A moment later, two of Acosta's men sprinted around the administrative building, en route to Second Platoon's position. Second Platoon had been assigned the mission of taking down the detention and manufacturing facilities housed behind its own fenced perimeter. The intel provided by the enigmatic Lauren Hunter indicated that more than ninety percent of the youth doing time in Tranquillity Base were never selected to go into the mind-control program, Project Monarch. The Nazi ghouls were looking for a very specific kind of troubled teen, one with a history of physical and sexual abuse. Youth with that kind of background came on board already a splintered personality.

The majority of teens were sent to the detention camp where they spent their year enduring rigorous discipline, moral "reeducation," and hard labor in the manufacturing plants and tobacco fields. Second Platoon did a fast-rope insertion into the middle of the compound and quickly took control. Its follow-on mission was to turn the detention facility into a temporary prisoner containment area. The Rangers separated the youth from the staff and were now taking in the captured prisoners.

Bolan made a radio call to his men for a situation report.

"This is Striker. What's your sit-rep?"

McCarter answered the hail. "We've got eyes on the bunker, Striker. No visible activity. Over."

"What's your location?"

"Take the road from the front gate and move toward the airfield. Look for a T-intersection just before the airfield. Take it. We'll be looking for you."

"Roger. I'll be bringing Third Platoon with me. ETA five mikes."

"Roger."

The Executioner stood. "Lieutenant, get your men together. We're moving out."

The lieutenant nodded and called his squad leaders to him for the preplay huddle. All aboveground objectives had been taken. No loss of equipment or personnel. All that remained was Objective Antares—the bunker. The real rat's nest in this place lay two hundred feet beneath the surface.

The battle to liberate Tranquillity Base hadn't yet begun.

11

Two hundred feet
beneath Tranquillity Base

McCarter put the finishing touches on the ring
charge adhered to the elevator door at the bottom of
the shaft. The explosive rope described a huge man-
size oval. The detonator was radio-delayed, and everything was ready to go.

"That's it, mate. Let's open this bloody can."

Bolan was crouched next to him. The self-
adhesive, highly sensitive listening mike was stuck
to the door, and the Executioner was gauging the
size of the force on the other side by the sounds the
enemy was making. At least a squad, armed to the
nines.

This was going to be a pitched battle, sure.

Bolan nodded and broke down the listening post.

Schwarz and Blancanales were above, looking
through the open escape hatch in the ceiling of the
elevator car. A rope with knotted handholds posi-
tioned every two feet dangled through the escape
hatch, and McCarter went up first. The two Able
Team commandos grabbed on to his assault vest
once McCarter's head and shoulders were through

the hatch and yanked him up the rest of the way onto the roof of the car. Overhead was two hundred feet of claustrophobic darkness and a little rectangle of light at the top with ant-people silhouettes peering down the shaft at the Stony Man warriors.

Bolan shimmied through the hatch and was halfway onto the roof before his three friends could get a hand on him to help. "Hunker down," he ordered. "It's going to be a big boom."

"Yeah," Blancanales groused. "This guy likes to overdo it."

McCarter grinned. "It's not worth doing, mate, if you don't do it right."

The four men pressed themselves into the two corners of the shaft farthest from the blast. They squatted, stuffed foam-rubber plugs in their ears, then opened their mouths to equalize pressure and prevent their eardrums from being ruptured. When they were ready and braced, Bolan told McCarter, "Do it."

The Briton had a little black box in his hand, with a single red button and a collapsible antenna telescoping out.

McCarter yelled, "Fire in the hole!" and pressed the button.

The ring charge went off like concentrated Armageddon. A blinding flash lanced through the roof hatch like a magnesium sun, and a concussion wave that was like living through a brawl in a biker bar compressed into a few pummeling seconds.

The boom and brilliance were replaced with the heavy-caliber chop of a .50-caliber machine gun accompanied by at least half a dozen 9 mm submachine guns. The interior of the elevator was being hosed down in a hailstorm of metal-jacketed death.

Bolan moved to the open hatch and dropped onto his belly.

"Hold my legs," he said.

McCarter and Schwarz wrapped their arms around a well-muscled calf, and the Executioner dropped through the hole upside down to get a quick eyeball of their opposition. The oval breach was almost laser perfect; the alcove beyond was gray with smoke and cordite. He could see whitish figures beyond, behind a short wall of stacked sandbags, and the winking globes of muzzle-flashes. Incoming rounds whined and ricocheted in the compartment around him. The enemy was too far away from the door to make a good grenade toss; the soldier needed something with some range. He quickly estimated the range and angle necessary to neutralize the obstacle.

The Executioner tucked back up before any of the enemy troops could target him. McCarter and Schwarz pulled him back onto the roof.

Bolan touched the throat mike. His radio was tuned into the Ranger tac net.

"Lieutenant, I need you to send down one of your soldiers with a LAW."

"Get out of the way. He's coming down now."

The commandos backed away and a couple seconds later, a Ranger came whizzing down one of the cables on a fast-roping slide to the bottom. He had on a pair of white Army-issue leather work gloves to protect his hands from the friction burn that would have seared the skin off his palms on the two-hundred-foot ride to the bottom of the shaft. He had an M-16 slung over his shoulder and an emptied rucksack with four LAW tubes poking out from under the top flap.

Schwarz quickly plucked the LAW rockets out of the rucksack and handed one to the Executioner.

"I ask for one and get four," Bolan said, "Rangers, always exceeding the damned standards."

"All the way, sir!" the Ranger replied proudly.

The Executioner pulled the pins out on both ends, dropped the covers and extended the launch tube. He knelt by the open hatch, got down on his chest and maneuvered the tube through. He held the launcher with the firing switch cupped in his fingers, keeping the weapon out of sight near the ceiling, and adjusted the firing angle by eyeball, getting it just right. Then he lowered his arm to clear the top of the breech and clenched his fingers tightly, squeezing down on the firing switch.

The rocket motor ignited with a shotgun boom, and the warhead streaked down the corridor in front of a smoky comet tail. Bolan's guesswork was uncanny. The 66 mm rocket impacted nearly dead center of the sandbag barricade, right under the jutting barrel of the .50-caliber machine gun. The explosion turned the barricade into a fiery sandstorm and the crew-served weapon into white-hot shrapnel. The enemy troops hunkered down behind the sandbags were pulped and violently ejected from physical existence into whatever lay on the other side of death's door. The back-blast from the LAW scorched the rear wall of the elevator and tattooed the brushed stainless steel with rings of heat discoloration.

Bolan released the launch tube, stood, then

dropped through the battle-fogged portal into the elevator compartment. He unslung the M-16/M-203 combo and shouldered the weapon, then crept into the hazy alcove as the other Stony Man warriors, followed by the Ranger, jumped through the escape hatch and hugged the walls to each side of and behind the Executioner.

The machine-gun nest was a smoking wreck, and the men manning it were mostly in pieces.

Bolan scanned the small-arms inventory scattered around the floor. Other than the .50-caliber machine gun, there wasn't any heavy-duty armament to defend the place.

Bolan put a call in upstairs. "Lieutenant, start sending your men down. We've established a foothold down here and have eliminated the first line of resistance."

THE TWO M-60 TEAMS WERE SENT to the head of the pack; the high-velocity 7.62 mm NATO round would make short work of the Kevlar body armor some of their opponents were wearing. Bolan and the Stony Man warriors made up the rest of the point assault element. The balance of the platoon trailed twenty yards to the rear, ready to reinforce, in two files on each side of the corridor.

It jogged to the left into a straightaway for about twenty-five yards before turning back to the right again. Bolan halted the advance just before the right turn and crouch-walked to the corner to take a quick look at what was waiting for them around the bend.

The Executioner poked his head out quickly at groin level and was greeted with a blazing hailstorm of hot lead. He jumped back and flattened against the near wall. Even in the brief glimpse he had, he saw all he needed to see.

Bolan waved his men and the M-60 gunners forward. Bullet strikes were still whining into the far wall even though there was no target to shoot at.

Bolan briefed the soldiers. "Looks like there's a big cargo bay in there. They've got a line of metal shipping crates just inside the entrance, which they're using for cover. Give me one of those LAWs."

Schwarz unslung a LAW and handed it over. While the Executioner prepared the light antitank weapon for firing, he outlined his scheme to the two Ranger M-60 gunners and their two AGs. The two AGs were heavily burdened by roughly one thousand rounds apiece of belted ammunition in boxes dangling from green gauze lanyards that crisscrossed their chests. Each AG also had a spare barrel bag looped over his shoulder and more ammo in his rucksack.

The Executioner said, "I'm going to fire this rocket right into the middle of their barricade. Once that explosion goes off, I want these two sixties down in that corridor firing at anything on two legs to your front. I want fire superiority fast. We're going to maneuver far enough into the cargo bay to set up good covering fire to allow the platoon to get inside and begin flanking whatever else they've got in there. Understood?"

The four Rangers said in unison, "Hooah, sir!"

"Get down and wait for the back-blast to clear," Bolan ordered. Then he shouldered the rocket launcher, matched the sight picture he wanted to memory and hopped out sideways into the open. He clutched down on the firing toggle, and the whizzer flew true dead to center mass and tossed the crates and enemy straight to fiery Hell as the detonating warhead parted the men like Moses parting the Red Sea.

Bolan dived prone as the rocket left the tube and yelled, ''Get those sixties in position now!''

The two teams hugged the walls running low and aggressively, and dropped behind their guns several yards in front of the Executioner. PFC Robert Curtain and his counterpart on gun two had the first belt fed into their guns and were preparing the ammo in the next box to be linked with the end of the first belt. The guns found their ranges by walking tracers onto targets. The gunners traded off firing precise 6- to 9-round bursts, and Curtain was laying out the asbestos mitten and spare barrel while hot brass and chain link rattled against the wall, punctuated by daisy-chained anvil booms and the jackhammering of the bolt.

The Executioner pushed off the floor, swinging the M-16/M-203 to his shoulder, and commenced shelling a mix of airburst and groundburst high-explosive rounds into the cargo bay. David McCarter was armed with one of the bomb chuckers, as well; his contribution was to add Willie Pete grenades to the mix and double the explosive firepower going downrange. Schwarz and Blancanales augmented the metal storm of the two sixties with short bursts from two Uzi subguns.

''Attack!'' Bolan shouted.

The AGs scooped up the spare barrel, bag and mitt as they jumped up with their gunners, supporting the ammo belts in their free palms. The two sixty teams rushed forward five paces and dived to the floor, reinitiating immediately. The new firing position opened up more of the right and left fields of fire into the cargo bay, revealing clusters of adversaries using the stacked shipping containers as cover. More gunners sprinted around crates in the far left sector, coming from somewhere out of view. The M-60 teams worked methodically and accurately, firing bursts that blew the new arrivals backward onto the floor.

The Executioner ran like a linebacker straight up the middle into the cavernous cargo bay. He weaved inside about a dozen yards and dropped behind a four-plex of metal containers. McCarter took position behind a neighboring arrangement. The two men stood at the same time and fired the grenade launchers on high arcs, sending two 40 mm rounds sailing over the large stack of crates toward the charging enemy. There was a clap of thunder, and several smoking corpses became airborne. The disruption in the flow of reinforcements was momentary and lasted only as long as it took for shrapnel to clear. The two M-60 teams were clear of the corridor and inside the bay, setting up machine-gun positions to cover the infiltration of the platoon.

The sheer size of the underground cargo bay was only now sinking in as Bolan eyeballed the area, looking for the strong point that had to be identified and neutralized ASAP. The huge bay described an elongated hexagon. The complex branched off in six places from the central hub of the cargo bay at each point of the hexagon. The man-made cave was as big as the Houston AstroDome. Three-quarters of the floor space was occupied by the large metal shipping crates, palleted and stacked in dozens of towering rows with aisles wide enough for forklifts. The forklifts were abandoned all over the cargo bay, their crews barricaded in the Quonset hut of the motor pool.

Drug processing was obviously a very big slice of this operation, and if even one-quarter of this black cargo represented drug supplies, Tranquillity Base was mainlining a large portion of the country with flake and crank. With the street flow of drugs increasing every year, Bolan wondered how much of the DEA was compromised by the Nazi conspiracy.

Blancanales and Schwarz joined Bolan and McCarter, popping off short bursts at targets of opportunity as the two Stony Man commandos jigged between crates for cover. The Rangers were storming into the cargo bay, fanning out into covered positions going right and left out of the corridor, laying down lethal bases of fire, pinning down oncoming enemy troops while leapfrogging fire teams moved in for the kill.

Bolan waved his men in to join him. The three Stony Man warriors ran low to his position.

The Executioner said, "We have to nail down where all these troops are coming in from. If there are enough of them down here, they'll just keep mobbing us until we run out of ammo and have to go to bayonets."

"We should have called up the whole bloody battalion," McCarter quipped.

Bolan nodded in agreement. "Yeah, but we didn't so we've got to make do with what we've got. Let's find that strong point and concentrate the battle there while we've still got a toehold down here."

The four black-clad commandos ran deeper into the vast cargo bay in a file, with Bolan at point. Grenades boomed in the background, small arms rattled continuously and the cries of the wounded and dying added the human chorus line to this symphony of destruction. The soldiers were traveling a large aisleway up the center of the cargo bay that ran perpendicular to the rows of stacked containers.

Over the tac net, Bolan heard the Third Platoon leader calling above to the First Platoon leader on the airfield to send down all the troops he could spare to help reinforce. First Platoon reported that a large freight elevator was discovered in the burned-out hangar, and two squads were coming down to join the fierce fighting. Second Platoon committed an additional two squads. Now they had a whole Ranger platoon in reserve on its way down.

With any luck, it'd be enough.

The Stony Man contingent stumbled onto the enemy strong point five-city-block-size rows into the cargo bay. At the fifth intersection, Bolan halted his team at the danger area and peered around the corner, looking right and left. Down the fifth row to his left was another huge rectangular portal. Enemy gunners by the dozen were rushing noisily through the open blast door, and all were armed with M-P5s and lots of ammo. None seemed to be toting rocket launchers, which was a big plus.

In the subdued bluish lighting coming from whatever was beyond that blast door, walking like a Titan among lesser beings, was the head of the lab facility. There was the fish that needed to be bagged. Bolan pulled his head back and said, "Okay, the leader of this den of vipers is in front of the door the enemy troops are coming out of. If the opportunity presents itself, we capture him. If not, we kill him."

"What's the play, mate?" McCarter asked over his shoulder.

The Briton was pulling rear security and was oriented in that direction.

Bolan didn't answer. He was busy looking around the vicinity for anything that could help them turn the tide quickly. On the other side of the fifth row, stalled out in the middle of the aisle that the Stony Man warriors were traveling, was a yellow forklift. The forks were raised halfway, supporting four of the big metal shipping containers on a pallet. Those crates made excellent cover for a driver.

And Bolan had an idea.

"David, you've got the Claymores and C-4, right?"

"In my kit."

"Okay, we're going to cross this intersection like a danger area. Standard drill. On the far side, you guys are going to pull security while I cook up a little surprise."

His teammates nodded their acknowledgment, the three of them flint-eyed professionals.

Bolan dropped prone and inched forward until he

had a good view of the activity downrange. His tight-fitting combat blacksuit and war paint made his image melt into the obsidian-black floor. Colonel Gabriel Aquarius stood inside the huge door, gesturing grandiosely, giving orders or reciting Shakespeare. He pivoted and strode deeper into the room. His men, double-timing out of the wall, were focused on the sights and sounds of the battle that they were moving out to join.

The Executioner leaped forward like a spring-loaded jaguar and sprinted low across the danger area, in full sight. Nobody was looking. He dropped prone again on the other side and covered Blancanales as he came across. McCarter cut in front of Schwarz and went across next under the cover of Blancanales's watchful muzzle. McCarter tapped Bolan out and took over security of the front. The Executioner uncinched the straps on the rucksack the Briton had on his back. Gadgets pulled in the rear; he and Blancanales molded into the floor and covered the rear and flanks.

Bolan reached into the rucksack and pulled out three Claymore mines, a block of C-4, four radio-detonated fuses, a roll of tape and a length of 550 parachute cord.

He used the OD-green duct tape to fasten each Claymore mine to the face of the shipping containers with a big X of tape. Satisfied that the mines were secure, he armed them with three of the radio fuses. He jumped up behind the wheel and uncoiled the 550 cord, and, using his combat knife, cut off a four-foot length. He tied the cord to the steering wheel with a prussic knot and left the free end unsecured.

He dropped back to the floor and went to the rear of the forklift, wedging the block of C-4 between the propane tank and the body. He penetrated the plastique with the pencil fuse and got back up behind the wheel.

Bolan started the engine and released the parking brake, saying to McCarter, "Detonate this bomb when it gets inside the blast door."

At the Briton's nod, Bolan applied the brake and shifted into Drive. Schwarz and Blancanales got out of the way. He tossed his M-16/M-203 to Schwarz. "Hang on to that for me."

He didn't need to be fumbling with an assault rifle when he bailed out.

The Executioner revved the engine and let the brake go. The forklift jumped forward, and he cranked the wheel sharply, jerking the forklift to the right and down the center of the fifth row, aimed directly at the center of the open blast door. He quickly tied off the steering wheel to the column with a round-turn and two half-hitches. He pulled his med pack off his vest and used it to wedge the accelerator. The Executioner stayed aboard long enough to make sure the forklift was going to steer true, drew the Beretta and jumped off.

Enemy gunners raced toward the oncoming forklift, firing on the run. Bullets sparked off the face of the crates and front of the forklift. Bolan drilled the duo at the head of the pack, knocking them off their feet. He triggered two more rounds into the charging force. The forklift was almost at the open blast door, and the Executioner was closer than he wanted to be when those explosives went off.

He turned and ran. As enemy weapons fired on full-auto behind him, one of the gunners found his range, and four rounds stitched Bolan across the back, feeling like supersonic baseballs on impact. The ballistic body armor that he wore under his assault vest deflected the bullets, but every foot-pound of energy was telegraphed into his back. It was like being hit from behind by an out-of-control city bus.

Bolan was pitched off his feet and driven to the floor on his chest. He fought to get his breath as his vision popped with purple star clusters of pain. He realized that the Beretta wasn't in his gun hand anymore, and he blinked to regain some focus, looking for the weapon around him.

The three Stony Man specialists were out from behind cover, returning heavy return fire. Bolan spotted the pistol, gleaming on the floor about ten feet away. He scrambled for it.

The forklift bulldozed forward, locked on target. Two of the enemy jumped aboard and were trying to free the steering wheel when the rolling bomb trucked through the blast door and into the designated kill zone.

Bolan heard McCarter bellow, "Fire in the hole!" and then the world was swallowed whole in flash and noise. The soldier felt the shock front go over him like a wall moving at the speed of sound, then he found himself in a hurricane of smoke, whistling debris and seared body parts. He covered his head with his arms and hoped that he'd still be alive when the storm passed.

The Executioner had to have momentarily

blacked out, as his next real memory was that of being gingerly rolled onto his back.

"Shit, he better not be dead," Blancanales said.

Bolan opened his eyes warily, blinking away the grit of combat.

McCarter was leaning over him, with the two Able Team warriors clucking over his shoulders like mother hens.

"Mack, are you all right, mate?"

Bolan tried to grin, but it came off like a grimace. "Yeah. Never been better. Am I still in one piece?"

Gadgets laughed. "Yeah, and you're one piece of work! You are one crazy guy!"

Bolan nodded and got to his feet gingerly, assisted by McCarter, testing his limbs to make sure nothing was broken, pulped or otherwise seriously injured. He seemed no worse for the wear.

The Executioner was still very combat capable. He retrieved his Beretta and holstered it. Schwarz handed back the M-16/M-203 saying, "Needs a new magazine. I used it to lay some of those bastards out, since my Uzi rounds just bounce off them."

Bolan dropped the empty magazine, plucked a fresh one off his assault vest and slammed it home. He notified the Ranger commander over the tac net that enemy reinforcements were no longer forthcoming and to mop up the force that was left.

The Executioner held his assault rifle at the ready, turned to face the smoke-and-fire-wreathed blast door and said, "Let's see what's behind door number two."

THE LARGE ROOM inside the blast door looked like the first ring of Hell. The only light in there came from the burning wreck of the forklift, which created ominous, shifting shadows that made the carnage all the more surreal. The overhead lighting panels were obliterated; wires and power cables dangled like animated tentacles, snapping and popping with live electricity. Some type of desk or console station had stood in the middle of the room but it was completely gone now, blown right out of the floor in the violence of the blast. There was no telling how many of the enemy gunners were caught in there when the bomb went off. Bolan tried to determine if the ringleader's remains could be visually identified, as he'd had only a brief glimpse of the man. The entire wall of the security station facing the Claymores was cratered, and if the man had been standing in front of it, Bolan might not find evidence that the man had even existed.

The open blast door into another tunnel might suggest otherwise, and Bolan's combat sense leaned in that direction.

The Executioner nodded at the yawning maw glowing an eerie low-key blue, which was all that was necessary to tell his men to flank both sides of the opening and cover his entrance.

The tunnel ahead didn't deviate at all from a straight line, and the soldier couldn't see the end of it. All he could hear was the hum of air-conditioning. If the head of the enemy force was still alive, he had a head start that demanded swift pursuit.

Bolan kept a mental count every time his left foot struck the steel-plate decking, and the corridor ended up being just over three hundred yards in length—over three football-field lengths with an identical closed steel door on the right and left every five yards. If each of these cells held a programmed teen, there were 120 human time bombs being cultivated behind those sealed doors, 120 steps closer to a total takeover.

The Republic wasn't going to fade into the night without one bloody, ugly fight.

Mack Bolan would see to that.

The corridor ended with an open watertight hatch. The soldier jumped through the oval opening onto a narrow catwalk suspended in space inside a large grotto. The overhead fluorescent strips illuminated milky stalactites jutting like fangs from the bare rock ceiling. He heard the water before he saw it.

The catwalk cut ninety degrees to the left and dropped in a zigzag staircase fifty feet to an empty dock. The Executioner loped down the stairs and stared down the natural tunnel and a flowing river.

Someone had gotten away.

THE REINFORCING Ranger platoon linked up with the defenders of Third Platoon and finished off the remaining enemy gunners quickly. A branching tunnel off the main hub was discovered to be a huge salt cavern housing a drug-processing and -packaging operation that could produce tons of flake and crank for street sales. A billion dollars in street sales was seized and destroyed with C-4 and incendiary grenades, and 110 teenagers were liberated.

Mack Bolan emerged from the underground Hell with a new enemy identified. He had thought he'd seen every permutation, every variation possible in the genotypes of Animal Man.

He was wrong.

While evolution meant the universe was constantly improving, on the upward spiral into infinity, something else parallel but retrograde was also hard at work, upgrading the stock of its brood, hell-bent to create a special breed of man and tip the cosmic scales forever in favor of entropy on this testing ground known as Earth.

And standing there on the edges of evolution and devolution, toeing the line on the frontier was one chosen man, Mack Bolan.

And for the moment, his side was winning.

EPILOGUE

Joe Newport emerged from the woods almost six miles southeast of Tranquillity Base. He was scratched all over by the tangle of vegetation, his feet were throbbing and he was soaked with sweat. He had no idea that this kind of cross-country evacuation would be such a brutal marathon of endurance and demand the gut-wrenching will necessary just to keep putting one foot in front of the other.

The physical shriek that his body was making was nothing compared to the thirst. He was starting to see little blobs of light floating in front of his eyes, and he knew that he was going to stroke soon.

He stumbled out onto the county road and collapsed to his knees.

All he could think about was water.

And then he fell into a black hole.

The splash of cold, cool water hitting the back of his throat snapped him back to earth, and he seized the plastic jug of water from the hands of the good Samaritan he couldn't see in the semidarkness of twilight. He swilled down half the gallon of water in gulps that brought him back from the edge of oblivion.

It took him another ten minutes of sipping and

breathing deeply before Newport felt energetic enough to stand again. His savior waited patiently for him to recover without talking.

When Newport was up to it, he followed the old man to his white Ford Ranger, keeping what was left of the water with him.

The quiet old man pulled the truck onto the two-lane road and turned on the headlights.

"Do you need to go see a doctor?" he asked.

Newport shook his head. "No. Drop me off at a motel."

"Yup."

Newport took another drink of water. God, it was good to be alive.

Before he could think about what he was doing, he pulled the nine-month-old pack of cigarettes out of his breast pocket. The plastic-wrap had preserved the smokes from being ruined by his sweat-soaked shirt. He shook out the cigarette he'd been lipping neurotically day after day since quitting and considered what he was about to do.

He looked at the old man's profile in the spill light from the dash.

"Mind if I smoke?"

The old guy shrugged without looking at him.

"Just roll down your window."

Newport punched the dash lighter and pulled out the ashtray.

The first pull off that lit cigarette was harsh, but it was like paradise.

It was good to be alive.

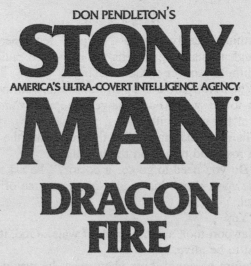

Take
2 explosive books
plus a
mystery bonus
FREE

End game begins for rogue arms dealers....

DON PENDLETON's
MACK BOLAN®

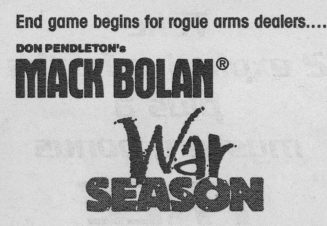

America reels in horror and shock when terrorists slaughter hundreds in Philadelphia, using a prototype weapon of megadeath called the Annihilator. The blood trail leads to a private arms dealer on the U.S. military payroll, selling hardware off the books. Mack Bolan's orders are sanctioned by the President and to the point: take down Amazon arms!!!

Available in September 2000 at your favorite retail outlet.
